WEIRD HORROR
No. 3

WEIRD HORROR 3
Fall 2021

PUBLISHER
Undertow Publications
1905 Faylee Crescent, Pickering
ON, L1V 2T3, Canada

Undertowpublications.com
WeirdHorrorMag@gmail.com

EDITOR
Michael Kelly

STORY PROOFREADER
Carolyn Macdonell

LAYOUT
Vince Haig

OPINION
Simon Strantzas

COMMENTARY
Orrin Grey

BOOKS
Lysette Stevenson

FILMS
Tom Goldstein

COVER ART
Fernando JFL

**COVER AND
MASTHEAD DESIGN**
Vince Haig

INTERIOR ART
Dan Rempel

WELCOME to issue #3 of **Weird Horror.**

From March 1 through to April 15, 2022, we will be open to submissions of fiction for issue #5. We will open in September 2022 for issue #6.

.

FICTION GUIDELINES

For issue #4 (Spring 2022) Weird Horror Magazine is open to fiction submissions from September 1 through October 15. Submissions must be original and previously unpublished anywhere, in any format, on any platform. Please do not query about reprints.

It may take the full submission period to respond. Simultaneous submissions are welcome. Please inform us if your story is accepted elsewhere. No multiple submissions. Please send 1 story.

We are actively seeking new and underrepresented voices.

We accept submissions from anyone, regardless of race, gender, or sexuality.

We are seeking pulpy dark fiction in the weird fiction and horror genres of 500 to 6,000 words. (**Please respect our word counts. Query first for longer pieces**). Monsters, ghosts, creatures, fiends, demons, etc. Dark crime. Suspense. Mutants. Killers. Ghouls. Golems. Witches. Pulpy goodness!

Payment is 1-cent-per-word, with a $25 minimum (paid via PayPal) for first worldwide English-language rights, for use in the print and eBook editions. We ask for a 6-month exclusivity. Copyright remains with the author, and a contract will be provided.

Submit stories in Standard Manuscript Format as a Word document or PDF, and e-mail as an attachment to: WeirdHorrorMag@gmail.com

Please format the subject line of your e-mail thusly: Submission - Story Title - Author Name

Please keep your cover letter short.

Submissions sent outside the submission period will not be read.

Please query if you have any questions.

.

ADVERTISING

Get your unique brand in front of our unique readers!

A full-page ad is just $60 (U.S.) per insertion. A half-page ad is $40. Ad space is very limited. We reserve the right to refuse unsuitable material. Please contact us at WeirdHorrorMag@gmail.com.

| Issue 3 | Contents | October 2021 |

Welcome to the new pulp! Weird Horror magazine is a venue for fiction, articles, reviews, and commentary. Published twice yearly — Spring and Fall.

SIMON STRANTZAS ON HORROR

A THING OF EXTREMES

THE monster is used in different ways in horror fiction, but perhaps the two poles of monsterdom are: the monster as mortal threat; and the monster as metaphor. All uses fall somewhere within this spectrum—I suppose that spectrum being from least metaphorical to most.

Monster as mortal threat is the simplest of the two, and perhaps the easiest to understand because it resonates with us on a primal, emotional level. We fear death, and the monster is the agent of death. The mortal monster takes many forms, from the alien bent on swallowing us whole, to the serial killer who thinks in ways we can't understand. The monster here is the Other, and we will never understand the Other. This is why it's monstrous, why it's frightening. One cannot reason with the mortal monster. All one can do is fight or run and hope to not die.

Monster as metaphor operates on a different, more abstract and intellectual level. The monster here does not necessarily intend to harm you. The metaphorical monster is an idea, frightening only because it is something too raw or too tangled to present to the reader in a literal sense. The monster doesn't bring death, not always. This monster brings instead a reflection of knowledge we don't have and can't learn because that knowledge, presented nakedly, wouldn't be absorbed. So, instead, the monster is that knowledge, abstracted enough that we allow it past our initial walls and defences. We let the monster in under the portcullis because we don't realize it's a Trojan horse. The metaphorical monster means to do more than harm us. It means to remake us through revealed knowledge. In some ways, perhaps it's the more dangerous of the two.

But, as I suggested, these are opposite ends of the spectrum. Are there any mortal monster stories told in contemporary times that *aren't* metaphors to some degree? I wonder sometimes how aware some authors are of the metaphorical potential inherent in the creatures they dream up, those things that live at the extremes.

Because isn't that what every monster is? A thing of extremes? Whether it's a physical extreme—too large, too small, too ugly, too pretty—or an extreme in action or viewpoint, what we consider monstrous is that which is as far from "us" as possible—the Other now becomes ourselves exaggerated beyond recognition. Us in caricature. But there's also danger in this depiction of the monster. Showing us at our extremes potentially threatens to open minefields, especially when what is *us* is too narrowly defined. For exaggeration to work, there must be some baseline of what normal is, and all too often and for far too long that normal has revolved around Western ideals, most especially those centred around straight white men.

I'm not suggesting all monsters are limited because of this—the metaphor makes universal many concerns that affect more than just Western men—but it is still the case that there remains a very specific lens through which the world is being portrayed, and even if it's not blatant this worldview inherently defines as monstrous anything that deviates from the norm. This is how we end up with overweight monsters like Annie Wilkes, or mishappen monsters like Quasimodo. Would Dracula have been so terrifying were he from England and not some "foreign" country? Would a one-armed man still be the villain in both *The Fugitive* and *Twin Peaks* on television and in film?

So what do we do? How do we tell stories about monsters without giving in to our base human fears about people who don't conform to society's vision of normal? Perhaps it's best for writers to focus on universal extremes that don't single out a specific group. The monster made of too much love, the monster born of too much pain, the monster inhabited by too much anger. Or perhaps the issue can be solved by introducing as many new and different viewpoints into the genre as possible with the hope that this will dilute the one worldview with the many, and that diversity will mitigate the potential of any one overwhelming the genre. But in practice we know from experience that people are resistant to such change, especially when they are the ones who benefit most from the imbalance. We may never reach this aspirational utopia, so for now maybe the best course of action for writers is to tread carefully and with added awareness when it comes to monsters and make sure they aren't thoughtless exaggerations of real conditions that affect real people with real feelings. We must be aware of what our monsters are and why we consider them monsters, regardless of which pole of monsterdom they bend toward.

You can see, though, how this sort of potential trap is inherent in a genre that trades in fear. What we fear is what's different. What's other. But we needn't be fearful, nor should we. The monster is a valuable tool in generating that layer of abstraction needed to process complex ideas—namely what is our world and what is our place in it? I don't mean this in the conventional sense necessarily. There have been books written about how fictionalized horror helps us deal with real world horror such as environmental issues and war, but it also helps on a more philosophical level, helping the reader better make sense of the more existential threat their material selves present to the unseen world around them. Monsters help concretize these things and allow us to at times better understand them while at other times actively find ways to combat them. Or, on occasion, join them. In this way, the monster is as therapeutic as it is dangerous.

All that said, despite the added weight metaphor brings, it's almost incidental to the way the monster story works. Most readers see the monster as nothing more than the fur on its back, the teeth in its mouth. It acts in ways that betray our inner selves and fears, but we don't see it as such, not in the moment. When we find ourselves confronted by these impossible beasts, no matter how ordinary or bizarre, we feel the same things the characters about which we're reading feel. Excitement and dread. Fear and wonder. That's what makes a good monster, after all, and what keeps these creatures fresh no matter how old and decayed they are underneath those rotting features.

GREY'S GROTESQUERIES

ORRIN GREY

**YOUR EYES WILL LEAVE YOUR BODY:
COMING LATE TO *ULTRA Q***

"*For the next 30 minutes, your eyes will leave your body and arrive in this strange moment in time.*" So begins one of the Rod Serling-like voiceover intros to *Ultra Q*, a show I had never even heard of until just the last couple of years.

Like a lot of people my age, I grew up with Godzilla. The big lizard was probably my first favorite monster which, given that John Langan once called me "the monster guy," seems like a big deal. I watched Godzilla's exploits in flicks that were broadcast on some local channel Saturday mornings; owned VHS copies of *King Kong vs. Godzilla* and *Godzilla vs. Megalon*; pored over images of Godzilla and their foes in those orange Crestwood House monster books; even begged my parents to buy me a knock-off Godzilla toy from the gift shop at the Wichita Zoo—a toy that still sits on my shelf to this day.

Even then, though, the Godzilla films I watched were being beamed to me from another age. The ones I was exposed to were primarily from what is known as the Showa Era, the earliest batch of Godzilla pictures, made between 1954 and 1975, while I was watching them in the '80s.

With that background, I can't tell you when I first became *aware* of *Ultraman*, but it must have been early. I never watched the show when I was young, though. Ultraman's sleek, humanoid design appealed less to my child's sensibilities than Godzilla's spiny, squamous, reptilian silhouette. I think that, as a kid, I probably saw Ultraman himself as too much of a "good guy." He *fought* monsters; Godzilla *was* one.

That said, I probably *would* have watched *Ultraman*, and gladly, perhaps voraciously, had it been available, but we didn't get a channel that

showed it. I wouldn't see an episode until *many* years later, after most of the events of this column had already unfolded.

Fast-forward a few decades from that kid eagerly crouched on the deep-pile of my parents' living room watching Godzilla movies on a big, wood-paneled TV, and I see a black-and-white gif on Twitter. In it, a man hugs close to a rock face as the glowing eyestalks of a giant snail slowly rise to tower over him. It was basically everything I ever wanted to see in a show, all contained in the few repeated frames of that gif.

A little digging told me that the image was from a series called *Ultra Q*; a Japanese tokusatsu show that had originally been broadcast in 1966. Created by Eiji Tsuburaya, the special effects pioneer who was partially responsible for Godzilla, the show featured plenty of kaiju – which were, of course, popular in Japan at the

time – but was intended to ape American sci-fi shows like *The Twilight Zone* and *The Outer Limits*.

Unlike *Ultraman* and the rest of the half-century-long (and counting) franchise that would follow it, the protagonists of *Ultra Q* were just regular folks—recurring characters included a couple of pilots and a female reporter, played by Hiroko Sakurai, who reappeared as a different character in *Ultraman* that same year.

In the course of the series' 28 episodes, these regular people encountered decidedly irregular events—the original title of the series was going to be "*Unbalanced*." Often, these events involved giant monsters—usually, but not always, from outer space—but they also ran afoul of gigantic primordial plants, honey that caused creatures to grow to abnormal size, a girl who could astrally project, and, in perhaps the show's most overtly horror-themed episode, the

abandoned mansion of a baron who had transformed into a giant spider.

From that gif on Twitter, I tracked down *Ultra Q*, first on DVD from Shout Factory, later on Blu-ray from Mill Creek. Finally watching the series, which was thrown together under tight time constraints, often repurposing suits and props that had previously been used in feature films, was a decidedly mixed bag. Some episodes were too childish or grating, but when the show was at its best, it hit all of my buttons in a way perhaps no other television series ever has. Here was something combining the speculative thoughtfulness of *The Twilight Zone* with the rubbery antics of early tokusatsu cinema, not to mention a team of unlikely paranormal investigators.

In just about every episode, I was guaranteed some kind of weird monster, many of whom later reappeared and entered *Ultraman* lore, but I was

also treated to some surprisingly ambitious concepts. Take, for example, the time-jumping alien invaders in "Challenge from the Year 2020" or "The Disappearance of Flight 206," which essentially prefigures Stephen King's *The Langoliers*, with an extradimensional walrus in place of the chainsaw-jawed Pac-Man monsters of that TV mini-series.

Ultraman entered production at the same time as *Ultra Q*, and the two series premiered the same year. It's obvious, looking back across decades that are filled with subsequent *Ultraman* shows, which one took off the most. I picked up a bunch of the *Ultraman* series that Mill Creek has been releasing, too, but, at the time of this writing, haven't watched more than a few episodes. It's not that I don't enjoy them—I like the monsters and the models, all the tokusatsu stuff—but they aren't, for me, what *Ultra Q* was.

Part of it is that there's just something about the old black-and-white footage of shows like *Ultra Q* and the American sci-fi series it was emulating. Not just the stark, noirish chiaroscuro of shadow and light, but also that sense of looking at something from another time. Something beamed to you from the past and yet made to live in the here and now; the antiquarian bent that so typifies the ghost story.

Ultimately, though, it may be the very *presence* of that super-heroic central figure which ensures that *Ultraman* and all those series that follow it will be something altogether *different* from *Ultra Q*. In the *Dark Horse Book of Monsters*, first published in 2006, there's a loving paean to the classic Jack Kirby monster comics of the 1950s—another phenomenon that I came to late and that was, in fact, being published almost contemporaneously with *Ultra Q* — penned by Kurt Busiek and Keith Giffen.

In it, retired adventurer Riff Borkum is relating the story of his last thrilling escapade — traveling to the Himalayas in search of "Kungoro, the Monster of the Snow," while back home in New York, a different kind of story is unfolding.

The conflict with the strange monster is ultimately upstaged by the arrival of superheroes, making diegesis of what was

happening in the actual comic book marketplace, as the popularity of tights and capes comics edged out stories like the Kirby monster tales.

"Now the wonders *are* the heroes," Borkum says, in the story's melancholy final pages. "Saving the earth from despots, alien races and more. And mankind ... mankind just watches. And sometimes applauds." Words that may have been reflecting on a past gone by but that feel uncannily prescient more than a decade later, when superhero movies dominate a box office once controlled by other fare.

The sentiment echoes one of my favorite lines from any film, the one that gave my second short story collection its title. Boris Karloff, playing a thinly fictionalized version of himself in Peter Bogdanovich's *Targets* (1968), another near contemporary to *Ultra Q*, laments that, "My kind of horror is not horror anymore. No one's afraid of a painted monster."

There's a wistfulness to both speeches, but not necessarily condemnation. The world moves on, and we're lucky enough to be able to come late to some

things, even if we didn't grow up with them.

I have no doubt that I'll have fun with *Ultraman* and its various spin-offs, and there's no denying which series was more popular and influential. But, just as some part of my monster-loving heart is always with Kirby's four-color creatures and Karloff's "painted monsters," some part of me will always be traipsing through the black-and-white sets of *Ultra Q*, waiting for my eyes to leave my body and arrive in that strange moment in time ... .

FROM OCTOBER VINES

GORDON B. WHITE

~ CORDIALS AND PORT ~

IF you speak a word, the spell is broken. This is the first rule of a dumb supper.

So you walk silently backwards up the steps from the unkempt lawn to the sagging porch, Madison behind you going first to open the door and Selene in front, bringing up the rear. Cheeks pouched, lips pursed, each of you carries a tray covered with a white dust cloth into the old house.

Through the foyer, up the grand staircase, you three walk backwards, dragging your heels so as not to trip on the steps. You watch the back of Selene's head, the collar of her pale dress. You listen for the brush of Madison's hem when she reaches the landing. Down the hall, then, still hesitant as warped boards under damp carpet bend beneath your feet. Moonlight through the great window's empty panes paints everything blue and black except your white dresses and the cloth over your trays.

Then Madison stops. The door behind you groans open into the room you girls had set for supper earlier that afternoon. That was back when there was light and you could speak.

Madison, you, Selene: in that order you back into the room. The round table at the center has no cloth, but bears a clutch of dead candles and eight full place settings with seven empty chairs. The seat closest to the door, however, is already occupied.

Regina, completely covered by the thick white sheet, waits. Stiff linen creases pool shadows along the hollows of her face beneath and, in the dimness, her features are melting like wax.

Then Madison strikes the match. As candlelight fills and softens the pits of Regina's shroud, you can almost imagine that what lies beneath is furniture or a sack of laundry. But comfort is fleeting.

The inside of your closed mouth is beginning to burn; your tongue is numb and your gums prickle. The cool sting of alcohol swells with every inhalation through your nostrils as they are tickled, too, by dust and the first bloom of rot. So the three of you set your covered favors on the table and seat yourselves in predetermined order. Clockwise, it runs: Regina, empty, Madison, empty, Selene, empty, you, empty. Regina's sheet glows against the void of the door directly behind her.

Madison nods to Selene, Selene to you, you to Regina. Regina doesn't move.

Before each of you is a place setting done in mirror. Spoons and knife on left, forks on right. Bread plate and dinner spoon hover between empty glasses for water, wine, and after-dinner drinks on the table's edge.

Madison lifts her smallest glass, and you and Selene follow. You raise them to your lips and spit back the liqueur you have been holding without swallowing since you first crossed the threshold. The liquid is dark amber and bubbled with saliva, but its ghost still coats your mouth like sap.

You place your glasses down. The dumb supper has begun.

◆

You took the crooked steps two at a time and the landing at a sprint. Still, when you reached the room—the round table already draped in white linen and ringed by eight empty chairs—Madison's shriek had collapsed into sobbing. Selene stared open-mouthed.

Framed by a panel of setting sunlight through the window, Regina lay. Her eyes were bulged by broken capillaries, her tongue swollen, her throat clawed and bruised. Her honeyed ringlets spilled out like an illumination of the soul rising from the dead.

Although the dumb supper was yet hours away, none of you spoke.

◆

~ DESSERT ~

The dessert course is Selene's. Seated opposite and furthest from Regina, she is still in shock after finding the body. She bears the same wide-eyed, unseeing disbelief as when Madison first lumbered the corpse into the chair and covered it with the tablecloth. Even now, Madison has to wave multiple times before Selene registers that it is time.

Had it gone as expected, the dumb supper would have been simple. You would do it backwards; you would do it in silence; you would do it on Samhain. One by one, each girl would be joined by an apparition of her husband-to-be. That had been the plan.

Selene uncovers the dish before her: German chocolate cake. She takes up the gleaming pie-knife's wedge, then turns it backwards, gripping the blade. With the handle, then, Selene furrows out eight mangled portions. One by one, plates are passed and she shovels out the moist crumb like mud in the candlelight. Dessert is placed in front of every seat. The three of you raise the littlest spoons.

A dumb supper, in truth, is not so universally simple. In some places, the empty seats are reserved for spirits. In others, it foretells if you will die. Here, tonight, you three who remain believe it might reveal who killed Regina. This is why Madison insisted on proceeding.

So you take a bite of the ruined cake, the sweetness piling over top of the liqueur's still-sweet residue on your tongue. The steady slog of chewing pulses through your jaw, jostling the mouse bones in your ears and burying all other sounds except the whistle through your nose. You are watching Selene in the middle of your second mouthful, however, when her eyes go wide and her face drains. This freezes you, and then you hear what she hears.

In the hallway, something heavy is approaching. A pulsing drag, pause, drag, pause, grows louder as it reaches the black of the door behind Regina. A drag, then a pause just outside the frame.

An enormous worm's glistening pink head pokes inside, large around as your thigh. In the candles' flicker, you see bits of loam clinging to its reticulations like morsels of German chocolate cake. Neither Selene, nor Madison, nor you make a sound as the worm inches in, around the table clockwise and towards Madison, who remains still.

It crawls past Madison, then rears up to squirm onto the seat between her and Selene. Selene begins panting around her mouthful of cake, hyperventilating as the chair on her right creaks beneath the worm's weight and it loops one kink of itself around the headrest to assume a seated position. She is about to scream and break the spell, despite Madison's furious waving entreaties, when the thing happens.

The worm parts its lips to reveal a set of yellowed teeth, as broad and flat as ivory dentures. It pulls its skin's edges back into a smile, then dips down to gnash at the chocolate cake before it.

◆

Bradley must have known why you were walking down the road with a salad bowl. The old house was the only thing out that way.

He smiled, leaning from his car window. "Have you seen Regina?"

It was a casual question made strange by the distance from any explanation for his presence. A boyfriend's bored curiosity? Jealousy?

He grinned again, batted his lashes. Your heart fluttered and you felt sick. You shook your head, No.

"Is she up at that house?" he asked "Are you girls doing something naughty? Should I go take a look?"
You shook your head again.

~ ENTREE ~

Without looking at the worm to her left or Selene sobbing one seat past, Madison prepares to reveal the entree. She and Regina, it seems, were the best friends and the circle's center. Selene, you had suspected and have now confirmed, was merely an extra spoke to help the wheel turn.

You are not unsympathetic. You already knew that Selene would die unmarried. You didn't need the dumb supper for that.

Madison draws back the white cloth from the tray before her, untenting a roast chicken already stripped to the bone. It verges on a surgical marvel how cleanly she has pared the flesh away, as if an anatomical diagram, blown out and the minutiae labeled, has fallen onto a silver platter.

As Madison reconstructs the chicken slice by slice for serving, Selene weeps openly without speaking, chocolate dessert crusted at her mouth's corners. The shovel-toothed worm, too, has pieces caked in its crevices but otherwise grins eyeless at its empty plate.

By the time Madison has reassembled her Faberge roast, there is a creaking on the grand stairs. As she serves it like a jigsaw, the footsteps creep across the landing. The hall. Outside the door. You look up as your plate reaches your hand. A man-sized and man-shaped shadow looms behind Regina's shroud before the door.

Bradley, in a form, half-steps into the room. There is a dizziness to his features, a mélange of his eyes and mouth and a shifting of his limbs. It is not so much that he cannot settle on which way to stand, but more that reality has not yet settled on which of the overlapping versions of him stands there. Selene, poor girl, does not respond at all. Madison, however, stares mouth agape, and then turns to you. Her eyes ask, without speaking, if you have been found out. Then, the alternative blossoms: Is this what you have conducted the dumb supper to discover? Was it him?

As Madison stares at you over the worm which delicately nibbles a drumstick with its outsized teeth, you watch the swirl of Bradleys in the doorway split like oil on water. The inaccuracy of his features, the almostness of his gaze, everything resolves as the solid part—the real Bradley—falls back and staggers off down the hall. Down the stairs. The door slams below.

The aspect of Bradley which remains is a gossamer boy, a thin and diaphanous fancy. He smiles so wide, but his eyes are empty and have no lashes to bat. With silent steps, the ghost of him skirts to Regina's right and sits down in the empty chair between you two.

Smiling blankly, the specter saws away at the ghost of the chicken with transparent versions of his offhand silver.

Madison stares at you. Her eyes are saying, I told you, I knew it was him. She tilts her head to the door, questioning. But you shake your head.

You sweep a hand to the remaining dumb supper before you. The spell can't be broken before it ends.

"Food comes last, stupid," Regina said. "You know that."

Your cheeks burned as she laughed. You picked up your covered bowl, but Regina grabbed your wrist. "Don't," you would have whispered, but you held still as her dusty fingers slid up under the sheath and plucked out a round, ripe tomato. Past her fine lips, she popped the fruit between her teeth.

"You're leaving me to set up alone?"

You opened your mouth as if to answer, but she waved you off as she wiped the juice from her lips' corner.

"Maddy and Selene are coming soon. Don't bother hurrying."

~ SALAD ~

You cannot put tomatoes back on the vine. You cannot plant cabbage back in the soil or re-stem spinach. What is done cannot be undone; what is seen, not unseen; said, not unsaid. You wonder, as you unveil your salad with the crisp bed-lettuces and jewel tomatoes, if the others appreciate this.

You have only dipped the tongs hinge-first into the bowl when the first cavernous thump resonates downstairs. Even poor Selene stirs momentarily from her horror and the worm beside her quivers, its attention drawn. Only phantom Bradley beside you continues to eat his ghostly meal uninterrupted.

Madison looks to you, the fear in her eyes almost a delicacy. Your cheeks flush to think that you are the expert here. Then you realize she is focused on phantom Bradley to your left. Has she put together that at the dumb supper the seats are reversed from custom, with the woman on the right and her date, or fate, on the left? That this makes Bradley yours and not Regina's? But does she really think you would entertain such a union? Well, yes, he's rich. Handsome, too, perhaps. But none of this is where your interest lies as the dumb supper approaches its conclusion.

You flap out the green leaves and ruby tomatoes alongside juicy cucumbers and crumbled feta. No dressing, of course, as you couldn't jury-rig it back into the bottle. Your aim now is to serve everyone before the drumming on the stairs arrives.

Since there are only two seats left—the empty one to Regina's left beside Madison, and the one right between you and Selene—Madison takes her plate and rakes her salad in with a knife. Selene and the monstrous worm grind face-first at their plates, mindless, as the intruding guest's heavy step resonates down the hallway.

With everyone else chomping away, you take the final plate as the approaching clomp reaches the hallway's end. Madison and Selene and the worm roar through their courses, as if finishing before the new attendant can assume his spot might prevent his arrival. You, however, place yours down with the leaves and glistening tomatoes untouched. The others have too much left to eat, anyway, and cannot wipe away the juice from the last ripe tomatoes fast enough as the behemoth enters.

It is an enormous coffin, covered in dirt. It wobbles from end to end into the room under its own power. A gentleman obelisk, it waits at the threshold for just a moment. A heavy breathing rocks the lid out and in. Then it wobbles in, step by half-step, three inches at a time. The wheezing ebony casket stumbles around the table, past the empty chair between Regina and Madison. Madison. The worm. Selene.

Then, with a ponderous inhale, it collapses towards you but you don't even flinch as only inches away it crushes the chair between you and Selene into splinters.

The wobble of the table sends cold salad tumbling across its face.

◆

Fresh from October vines, you ran the tomatoes beneath the kitchen tap and placed them on the terrycloth towel to dry before adding them to the salad. Undressed, obviously.

"I don't know why you're doing this with them," your brother called from the living room. "Bradley, Regina's boyfriend, says they say you're weird."

You knew that. But you also knew they thought you knew weird things, too. Things like the dumb supper.

And you do. But you know better ones, too.

You inserted the hypodermic needle through the tomato's skin, just a perfect little hole, and plumped it full and juicy.

◆

~ APERITIF ~

Aperitif was to be Regina's, but your digestifs sit there, waiting. This is the dumb supper; the end is the beginning.

Poor Selene, already drained, died almost immediately. Draped across her coffin, her cooling weight keeps the lid from rattling. The worm, too, is slung over its headrest, purpling and tumescent as poison courses through its single vein. Madison, though, still thrashes willfully on the floor. She claws her throat as if to open it for air and, wildly flailing, grips the cloth covering Regina. She yanks it away to reveal Regina—the first and now final unveiling—yawning as black and empty as the doorway beyond.

Soon enough, however, even Madison stops moving.

Alone, you lift your aperitif, having come full circle. The liquid is still dark amber, pearlescent with saliva bubbles. You are contemplating its viscosity when the last guest appears.

You.

The you who enters is thin and gauzy, like Bradley's specter still blithely smiling on your date-side. You try to wave your doppelganger away; the party is already over and the killer revealed. Nevertheless, it seats itself on Regina's body's left.

Hollow-eyed and grinning, your ghost is sitting politely when the first splash of crimson light soaks the room. It washes ruby red, then bruise blue, then repeats. You rise and approach the window. Down below is a police car, lights flashing but siren off.

Two officers emerge and open the back to release their passenger. It's Bradley: the real Bradley, not your ghostly companion who split off from him when he intruded during the entree course. Your killer, then, and not your husband. You sigh. That makes more sense.

He points up to where the window frames you, so you smile and wave. As the officers stare, hands on holstered pistols, you raise a toast, the liqueur alternating red and blue as if unsure of its final form. Then you turn back to the dumb supper's remains.

Downstairs, the front door is kicked in. When they reach this room, the spell will be over, so you prepare. As they gallop up the grand stairs, you blow out the candles. As they reach the landing, you pick up a fork and spear one perfect tomato from your salad plate. In the flashing light it is the most brilliant red, then the dullest gray, blinking like an eye.

The men are racing down the hall as you hand your ghost the fork. The first officer inside tackles your double from its chair just as it bites down. Bradley and the other officer, taking in the full carnage, blanch. You smile and throw back your aperitif.

Your own deal is concluded, your spell completed.

You are vibrating. You are transforming. Darkness consumes you and then you are darkness. You are more powerful, less defined, than anything Regina, Madison, Selene, Bradley, or anyone else could have imagined.

In the gap between red and blue, you slip out through the darkness into the night. You spread your wings.

◆

You were pruning vines when the darkness spoke to you again from the shadows beneath the leaves. You pretended not to hear.

Regina, Madison, and even Selene, had ditched you again. But it was fine, you lied; more time to attend to these withered stalks. Your tomatoes were still unripe, but without the leeches they might be salvageable.

The darkness called you by name and you clipped a bit too far, nicking your fingertip.

"What do you want?" you hissed.

Your brother slid open the side door. "Telephone," he called out. "It's those girls."

"You," the darkness answered.

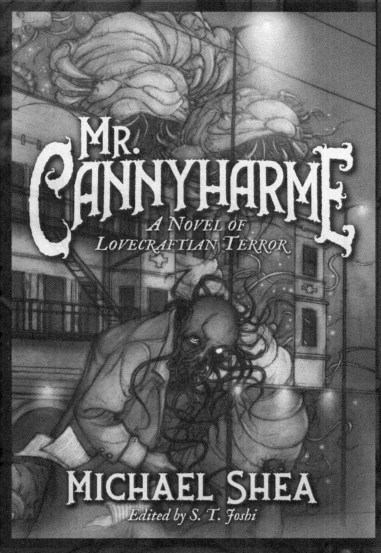

THE FOREST HAS NO IMMEDIATE PLANS TO KILL YOU

REX BURROWS

THE trail isn't easy to find, but trust me, it's there. Head north on Route 27 for about thirty miles. After the farmland has given way to forest, you'll come to a spot where the overhanging trees form a tunnel over the road. Stop there and park along the shoulder. To find the trailhead, you'll need to poke around in the brush until you find a length of rusted chain strung between two metal posts. There's a no trespassing sign affixed to a tree trunk but pay it no mind. No one has lived out there for a very long time.

The beginning of the trail is overgrown with scrub, so you'll have to push your way through at first. Don't worry, that will clear out soon enough. The canopy of leaves is too thick to allow much of an understory. At ground level, the forest is just ferns, moss, and huge trunks—oak, beech, poplar—holding up all that growth overhead. You don't encounter many trees of this size anymore, at least not in this part of the country. Nearly all of the woodlands were cleared for agriculture in the nineteenth century, and what you see today is regrowth on abandoned farmland. This forest, however, is true old growth. If you were strolling through a thousand years ago, it would look pretty much the same as it does today.

The trail meanders through the woods, but it doesn't branch or intersect with other paths. There's just the one way in and out. The only sounds you're likely to hear are the creaks and groans of branches and the crunch of dry leaves underfoot. The foliage should just be coming into peak autumn colors. You'll be tempted to keep your head tilted upwards, but don't neglect the forest floor. If you keep your eyes open, you'll begin to spot large fungi poking up through the leaf litter. They're roughly the size and shape of cantaloupes, grayish-pink with mazy, convoluted patterns furrowing their surfaces. You won't find this particular type of fungus anywhere else on the continent, maybe even the planet. They're what makes this forest truly unique.

Yes, they're edible, but I wouldn't recommend tasting them. I don't think the flavor would agree with you.

The trail ends in a wide, dim clearing. Far overhead, the branches arch together into a natural cathedral. The ground is nearly covered with the fungi—please be careful where you step—but you'll notice they're somewhat different from those you passed on the way in. These are fresher specimens, and many are still partially encased in flaking shells of bony material. As you approach the middle of the clearing, you may notice holes resembling eye sockets or even patches of hair still clinging to a few. Under normal circumstances, I'm sure you'd find this observation more than a bit disquieting. This is the heart of the forest though, and the space exerts its own peculiar psychological gravity. By the time you reach it, I expect all you'll be feeling is a sense of numb, stupefied wonder.

In the center of the clearing, you'll find a narrow shaft excavated into the soil. It's just the right width and just the right depth for you to lower yourself down and stand with your shoulders level to the ground. The walls of the pit are covered in a dense webwork of white threads. Did you pay attention in your biology classes? If so, you might recognize these fibers as fungal hyphae. The fungi's showier bits are above ground, but it's the inconspicuous hyphae that form the vast hidden bulk of the organism. They form a subterranean network that spreads throughout the forest's soil and connects into the tree's root systems, tying everything together. Once you're safely ensconced in your earthen socket, the hyphae will relax their grip on the black loam and allow it to crumble in around you.

Constraint is never a pleasant sensation. It tends to shake a body into awareness. It would be perfectly understandable if you experienced a momentary sense of alarm or even panic. Fear not, the forest has no immediate plans to kill you.

Yes, true, your body will be broken down into its component nutrients and absorbed into the soil. Waste not, want not. The forest's true interest is with the three pounds of spongy gray tissue encased within your skull. That part of you, the truest part, will live on for a very long time. The hyphae will already be insinuating themselves throughout your circulatory system, traveling upwards and eagerly pushing their way past the blood-brain barrier. You see, consciousness isn't just a matter of cells and tissues and chemicals. It requires a certain degree of architectural sophistication, and the fungi have never quite mastered the art of building the necessary structures. At least not without a template.

The process won't take long. You'll become aware of certain thoughts that might initially register as external. Alien. Other. This sensation will pass quickly, and your self-awareness will be subsumed into a greater whole. You won't retain much in the way of independent identity, nor will you miss it. You'll be engulfed within a massively pluralistic sentience, one that spans across species and miles and centuries. As I mentioned before, this is a unique and beautiful ecosystem. It's a great privilege to join it.

The forest isn't greedy. It's content to sit for decades at a time, alone with its thoughts. To ensure its continued survival and solitude, the forest sheds a continual rain of psychoactive spores. Once inhaled, they act to subtly influence behavior and deter interference. The forest occasionally requires a bit more of its neighbors though; think of it as an organ donation. Which brings us back to our little chat. You see, I'm not really here. There's not even a me. Your mind is simply trying to make sense of the jumbled packet of semiochemical information that you breathed in earlier today. Don't worry, you won't recall any of this when you wake up tomorrow morning. You'll just have a strong urge to take a peaceful hike in the country. You'll remember hearing about a secluded stretch of trail that would be perfect. You'll head north on Route 27 for about thirty miles, out past the farmland...

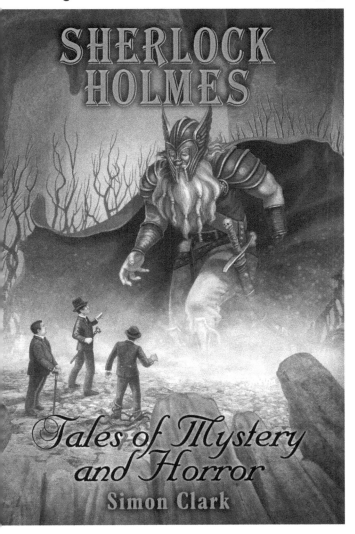

Rempel '21

FEAST

S.E. CLARK

For a moment the snow stops and through a gap in the clouds the moon shines like a hunk of ice in a highball glass. Silver washes across the window-sills and sparkles off the ornaments on the Christmas tree before fading to the dull orange light of a streetlamp. Henning struggles with a string of dead bulbs. He tests one and it shocks his finger. "Shit!"

Once he's sure neither he nor the tree are ablaze, he asks, "Are these safe? When did you buy these? They're ancient."

Connie doesn't look up from her sheaf of papers. "They're yours. You stole them from your mother's house after the funeral."

"I didn't—"

She peers over the top of the pages. "Your father's watch, your suit, and the sugar bowl too. You didn't want your sisters to have them."

"Oh, right," he says. "I tore my good pants on the bathroom window."

"You'd been invited. You could've used the front door."

"It was locked. They don't give keys to dead people. Ah—" He finds the dud in the string and replaces it with a fresh one. The Christmas lights glimmer among the fir branches. "That's better. What do you think? Connie?"

She clicks her tongue as she rifles through another stack and scribbles in the corner. Still in her sweatpants, she curls herself deeper into the couch; the piles of thumbed-through letters and research logs surround her like a fortress. And he's wanted to better understand what kind of doom-filled prophecy she's latched onto ever since he came across the rumpled leaflets laid out on the kitchen table, but it all went over his head. Sea level rise recorded in centimeters, urban flooding, coastal erosion, significant loss of habitat and life by 2050—every bit as dour as a book by Mother Shipton. Besides, 2050 was eons away.

When Henning steadies her pen with a finger-tip, Connie frowns.

"Sweetheart. You've been slaving on this project for weeks. Take a break. Get in the holiday spirit. Validate my decorating."

"You would've been one of those idiots who popped champagne on the *Titanic*." She pauses. "... It's a nice tree."

"Thank you." He kisses behind her ear and under her cardamom perfume lingers the sourness of cigarettes. "Have you been smoking again? You know it makes me wheeze."

"Are you telling me I stink?"

"Of course not," he says, nuzzling her shoulder until she chuckles and pushes him off.

Something about her seems burned out. Blue tints her lips and the circles under her eyes. He knows if he asks her why she'll dodge his questions, and if he fights her, they'll be late to the party. So he relents, leaves her a milkshake of vanilla ice-cream cut with an ounce of whole blood on the coffee table and changes into the Merhinger suit he pilfered in Illinois.

"What are you wearing?" He calls from the bedroom. "I want my tie to match."

"Your enthusiasm is misplaced. It's only a party."

"A *Paulfry* party, at the *mansion*. And I finally got an invitation. Well, you got the invitation but they added me as 'guest.' I heard he's bringing in a jazz band from Chicago. They worked with Jelly Roll Morton. Never did get to hear him live."

"So? You'll mingle with avarice and folly for an hour. People dance, gossip, fuck in the bathroom. All things I've done several times on several continents."

He pokes his head out of the bedroom. "Sorry I haven't lived as adventurous a life as you."

"Hen—"

He retreats to the mirror where an empty suit floats on air and she follows, turning him toward her so she can fix his tie. Below the window, carol-ers sing as the snow begins anew and gathers in the corners of the glass panes. It reminds him of sneaking downstairs to catch Santa Claus, only to find his parents dancing to the Savoy Christmas Special on the radio in the kitchen. This is the season of wonder, of trees growing indoors, of spiced wine and Pierniczki and points of light burning in the dark. On nights when Connie feels generous, they masquerade themselves among the holiday revelers in Boston Common, the shoppers and the bell ringers and the families with little ones swaddled in heavy coats. Sometimes he imagines what it might be like to walk with a child on his shoulders as they point out every illuminated snowflake and star.

But Connie sees everything as an indulgence or a hunting ground, or lately, something worse. Once, he asked her if there was any good news in all her models and projections, and she said New England was less likely to be swallowed by wildfires, so they were less likely to go up like kindling. Fire was not kind, especially to them. But there were other losses, other sacrifices to be made.

Her eyes linger beyond the glass of the window. "Someday it won't snow here," she says.

He doesn't speak, only runs a hand through her tangled hair and glances at the clock. If they don't hurry, they'll be late.

"Maybe," he says, "in time."

◆

The Essex Coastal Scenic Byway is aptly named: a long, winding road with the mansions of the nouveau-riche to the left and the brewing Atlantic to the right. The gabled Victorian of the Paulfry estate stands out among the new construction like an old dame. Golden light glows from the windows and the low thrum of music seduces partygoers as they walk up the grand staircase to the entrance. The doorman—a six-and-a-half foot gentleman with a brow ridge as steep as El Capitan—nods to the guests as he ushers them in. When Connie steps to the threshold, he bows and welcomes her in. The bell on the end of his striped hat jingles. Henning follows; the giant's hand lands like a slab of pork on the middle of his chest.

"Invitation only," he says.

"Oh, it's in my front pocket." Resting under the doorman's enormous thumb. The doorman sniffs.

"He's my escort," Connie says.

His brow lifts. Henning's surprised it doesn't cause an earthquake.

"My apologies, Ms. True." His hand retreats and he looks down his nose at Henning's crumpled jacket. "Come in," he says, flatly.

"I think he likes me," Henning says as he offers Connie his arm. She pats it and they walk through the foyer to the grand ballroom. He forgets the doorman's manhandling—how could he not, with the way ballroom twinkles, festooned with strings of light, velvet garland and greenery? Across the dance floor, a woman in a chartreuse tuxedo waves around her heel—red bottom flashing like a flag—as she leads a crowd in a carol: *Avec des jouets par milliers...N'oublie pas mon petit soulier!* The jazz band rolls through "Embraceable You" and the fae on the trumpet plays so sweetly that his gossamer wings flair on each crescendo. The women here have drenched themselves in sapphires and rubies and the men wear suits Henning knows cost more than he's made in his lifetime and after it. But it's the tree that amazes, all fifteen feet of it dressed in baubles and bows and yards of glistening fabric.

"Would you look at this?" he says, gesturing at a table set with crystal bowls of punch, cherries, oranges and ripe strawberries, "incredible." He pauses. "Damn. I forgot a gift for the host."

"He won't notice. Too self-absorbed, these simpering monsters," Connie replies as she tugs at something hidden in the bust of her blue gown.

"You drink this and tell me it's monstrous." He ladles out a glass of punch. The metallic scent hits and his mouth waters. The floating orange slices in the bowl have an arterial tinge. Just as he's about to comment on the unusual freshness, he knocks over the tray of a passing waitress and silverware falls to the floor. Something else, too—a small pink pacifier amongst the forks and spoons.

"I'm sorry," he says, reaching down to help as the waitress scrambles for it. He finds the pacifier first; his fingers brush against her hand and she flinches back as if electrified. Her eyes are clear, pupils huge. She's unglamored, unveiled of any illusionary magic. She knows what they are. Shame burns through him.

Connie yanks him up by the collar. "You'll draw attention to her," she hisses. "He's coming."

"Who?" he says, when a hand claps down on his shoulder and the bloody punch sloshes over the lip of his glass. The man appears at Henning's side as quick and silent as smoke.

"Me," the man says. "So you found a fresh one, Constance? You always did like them modern."

"Pleasant as ever," Connie replies.

"You're the one who finally accepted my invitation. Something about the party must have drawn you out of your hermitage."

"Yes. *He* wanted to go."

Henning clears his throat and offers his hand. "John Henning. And you're...?"

"Paulfry." His grip nearly crushes Henning's knuckles. "Stephen Paulfry."

Stephen-fucking-Paulfry, Henning thinks as the handshake breaks and he rubs the mark left on his palm by Paulfry's ring. The host seems lifted from a Lucky Strikes poster, suit immaculate and glossed hair greying at the temples. But something in his smile is pinched, unkind, and Henning grieves that he can't shove the gold ring down his throat.

The host scowls as the waitress reaches for the last spoon near his feet. He steps on it and she freezes. "What's this? Is she bothering you, Constance?"

Henning bristles. He opens his mouth and Connie elbows him in the ribs.

"I haven't noticed anything except your tree," she says, and with a few steps turns the host towards the glittering lights and places herself between him and the waitress. Paulfry's face relaxes, and as he brags about the price of decorations, the retinue swarms them in a haze of jubilance and booze. The waitress flees before Henning can slip her the pacifier. He sticks it into his pocket as the guests clamber around Connie like puppies.

It's surreal, watching the fingerprints of Connie's old life raise as the woman in the chartreuse tuxedo—"Imogene," Connie calls her—throws an arm over her shoulders. He knows Connie best bathed in moonlight, crouched in the field counting fireflies, cataloguing whatever wild places are left. She's as poised here as she is when examining vernal pools, except for the strain in her voice, the tightness of her mouth.

And then the attention of the crowd shifts and the guests fix him with stares that remind him of very eager dogs just before they bare their teeth.

"Where'd you find him, Constance?" asks a diminutive priest with a reedy voice.

"I'm from Illinois," Henning answers.

"A farm boy?"

"Oh, no. I grew up in Chicago. I sold merchandise door to door. Pools, gravestones, bibles—"

"A business man!" Paulfry snatches a glass of port from a waiter's tray. "What college did you go to?"

"I was recruited to play football at the University of Illinois, but the Crash happened, and my family had mouths to feed, so...Always wanted to go back, but, you know how life is."

"My parents were patrons of Harvard."

"Oh."

Imogene adjusts her lapel. "You played American football! Tight end?"

He blushes. "Halfback."

"How long ago did you turn him?"

Connie drinks from a flute of champagne. "About fifty years."

"A young one!" a guest says.

"A toy," whispers another.

"I'm very lucky Connie found me," Henning says. He feels her squeeze his hand as the guests glance at one another. Silence lingers for a moment before Imogene announces that her newest collaboration, a polka-grunge-garage band named *Stinky Bohemian Girl,* would be playing its maiden show at T.T. the Bear's. The partygoers fawn. The awkwardness drains away. He can't help but notice the rest of the staff now, how hard they try to remain invisible, how underneath the spice and perfume he can smell their fear.

"Let's go," Connie murmurs, but servers with tiny bowls of soup flank them before they can escape. There's nothing to do but eavesdrop on Imogene and the priest's argument.

"It's an arresting story, spiriting a child away in the middle of the night to avoid a slaughter," Imogene says, "but the innkeeper is such a puzzle. Tell me, Father Burke, did the innkeeper make it to heaven for doing the bare minimum?"

The priest caresses his balding pate. "I cannot say. Only God can truly understand our intentions."

"Well *I* wouldn't have let a poor woman give birth in a filthy stable."

"I'm sure all of us would have given up our very own beds," Paulfry says.

Henning tips the entirety of the bowl into his mouth and it dribbles at the corner. It's heavily spiced, but the meat tastes like soil. The guests snicker.

"Someone's hungry," Paulfry says. "You act like you've never had terrapin before."

Connie frowns. "Turtle soup? It's illegal to harvest here, they're endangered."

"Oh? Then I'll have to eat them while I can. You only get so many chances."

The crowd laughs and nods. Henning forces down the mouthful as Connie fumes.

"I propose a toast," the host says, holding his glass aloft as the other guests, except Connie, raise theirs, "to our great feasting."

When the crowd clinks their glasses, Paulfry upends Henning's punch and it splatters all over his lapel. The guests snicker as Henning stands helpless, bloody punch seeping into his shirt.

"Oh my!" Paulfry says as he grips Henning by the shoulders and turns him towards the ballroom, "Why don't you get cleaned up. Restroom's that way. Just put down your things wherever you like. Constance, let me show you my newest Monet—" and the group whisks her away before either can put up a fight.

Struggling through the clot of revelers, Henning ducks into a hallway lined with doors. The first yields a butler's pantry with hutches full of ceramics and silverware. The clamor of the kitchen staff echoes from behind a red door at the far end. The floor's a mess: an open crate of tangerines, a pile of muddy clothes, an odd-shaped something covered with paisley cloth. Henning steps in, searching for a wedge of lemon to take out the stain, when Something coos. Under the cloth—more like a shawl—Something wiggles. He hesitates, glancing around for witnesses and finding none, lifts the shawl. The baby in the car seat looks up at him and smiles.

"Huh." He drops the shawl and pulls it up again. The baby laughs. Kneeling down, he makes funny faces, a couple peek-a-boos, before gently pinching her nose. Two gold charms dangle from the collar of the girl's coat—a hand with two outstretched fingers and a diminutive, twisting horn.

"This must belong to you," he says, retrieving the pacifier from his pocket. He rubs it on his shirt before dangling it in front of her, and when she whacks it out of his hand, the pacifier falls into the folds of the shawl.

"So who do you belong to?" he asks. The child shoves her fist into her mouth.

There are, he's sure, a million reasons for this girl to be here. Outrageous childcare expenses. Bad parenting. As normal as finding the family dog in the middle of a house party. Who is he to judge, even if he had more self-respect than to abandon his own offspring just to kiss Stephen Paulfry's ring?

Behind the red door voices swell. Footsteps, squealing metal. Curious. Henning cracks open the door and peers inside.

When he was a boy in Illinois—back when he ate food for more than just pleasure—and the larder grew too lean, he took the family hound to the outskirts of the city and hunted rabbits. Sometimes his kills were not so clean and the hound would trot up to him with a screaming bunny in its mouth and he'd have to end the small beast's misery up close. He never forgot the whites of their eyes, the way they trembled between life and death.

He sees this now in the eyes of the naked man and woman in the cage. The man slumps against the woman's knees and stares at nothing while her lips mime supplications and the blood matted in their hair smells like wine. On the other side of the cage, two waiters argue over who will deliver them.

The woman's eyes find Henning's. They cross some invisible divide, the space between the wounded rabbit in the pasture, the hunter peering through his scope. He freezes, caught.

"Mia figlia," she pleads.

The waiters have decided and the loser throws a drape over the cage. He crosses himself and wheels it out of the kitchen.

Henning slowly closes the red door. Only when the lock makes a small click does he realize he's been holding his breath.

The child blinks at him as he flings open cabinet doors and drawers, searching for anything to conceal her. He can't take the car seat—they'll know, they'll stop him, of course they will—if not Paulfry then certainly the seven-foot ogre at the door. But maybe, while the guests are feasting, he can find Connie and slip out.

Someone's screaming in the ballroom.

He trips on the tangerine crate and kicks it. His toe crunches against the wood and he curses. Goddamn, that's a sturdy box.

Huh.

In the pantry, the car seat sits empty, tangerines strewn across the floor.

◆

The band breaks into "Smokestack Lighnin'" and the howling of the singer turns his skin to gooseflesh—if the child follows, she's sure as dead. The ballroom reeks; he holds back a gag with his tongue.

Everywhere he turns there's red: an arc sprayed on a white linen tablecloth and the marble floor, a handprint on a waiter's crisp shirt, a trail from bust to navel on a reveler's gown, uncountable hands, mouths. He hovers at the edges of the party, far from the empty cage, trying to spot Connie's blue dress. He finds her smoking a cigarette in front of the Christmas tree. Her hands are clean.

"Shit." She grinds out the cigarette on a sliver bell and flicks the butt into the branches. "I know I said I quit, but—where's your coat? What is that?" She nods towards the shrouded crate.

"Don't panic," he says, panicking. "We need to leave, immediately, right now."

Connie's brow furrows at the small, muffled giggle coming from the crate.

"Hen, what did you do?"

"You may have to break the doorman's nose. No, wait—"

Despite his whining protest, she raises the edge of the linen and looks into the crate. The baby, swaddled by a Merhinger jacket, sucks on the sleeve. "For *fuck's sake, John.* Put it back."

"No!" He pulls the crate away. "You saw what they did to those people."

"It's not your business."

"She's just a baby!"

"She's a libation, a nightcap."

"So was I, once."

"And I should have kept it that way, for your own good!"

"Lover's quarrel?" asks a voice. The iron scent of blood wafts between them as Henning's shoulders hunch, and he turns, shifting the crate from one side to the other. Stephen Paulfry tilts his head as he sucks on his fingers. "Oh please, not at Christmas."

"You've returned," Connie says, "joyous."

"The host needs to eat too." He digs at the underside of his thumbnail with an incisor, then points. "What's that?"

"This?" Henning replies as he gently jiggles the crate. "Nothing."

"It's moving."

The fabric creases as if gripped by tiny, searching fingers, and Henning shoves them down with his palm.

"It's a surprise—a gift."

Paulfry squints. "Open it then."

"N-no, I, well, have to check its freshness. I want it to be perfect." He sends a frantic glance towards Connie. "Isn't that right, sweetheart?"

Connie says nothing, but the tension in her face and the soft bite of her cheek reminds him of how she looks hunched over her reports and projections. The thin line of her mouth reads like an omen.

"Hm." The host steps closer to pinch the edge of the shroud.

"Is this one of my tablecloths?"

"Tablecloths, they're all the same."

"I import mine from Egypt." He shrugs. "Either way, I'm sure if you picked it out it is as perfect as it'll be."

He yanks the edge of the covered crate. It nearly pulls Henning off balance and he grips it tight. The teeth come out as they round on each other to play tug of war as nails loosen and wood splinters, until one good tug breaks the crate apart.

The baby tumbles out. Henning catches her by the ankle and uprights her against his chest as she screams. Now the whole ballroom has eyes on them and the drop of blood that glistens on her cheek.

They surround, jackals dressed in jewels, a green top hat, a priest's collar. Despite their feasting they still hunger. He sees only mouths, waiting. He turns to look for an escape, finds none. Connie is gone.

The girl chokes on her own sobbing and he tries to hush her as Paulfry advances, his steepled fingers pressed to his chin.

"You know, when we first met, I only thought you were stupid, not a thief. I *was* going to share."

"She's just a little child, for god's sake—have mercy—"

Paulfry stops, frowning. "Mercy? You're not taking it for yourself?" He snorts. "What, were you going to buy a baby carriage? How maternal, you're positively lactating." Laughter ripples through the circle of guests.

Henning swallows, throat dry, as the child whimpers. "Let her go, she's barely a mouthful."

Paulfry holds up a hand and the guests quiet. "The point of a delicacy is not that it fills you, it's that you can afford to have it. And I paid very well for our delicacies today."

He snaps his fingers. The doorman emerges from the foyer and makes his way through the ballroom, glamour wavering as tusks curl over his lips. The crowd fidgets in anticipation.

"The problem," Paulfry says, "with people like you is, somehow, you still think of yourself as a man. Maybe even a noble man, like that has value. But it doesn't. It does not matter. That child? She doesn't matter. And you—Jonah?—you don't matter as well, so no one will notice when you disappear."

And as the crowd readies to pounce, the stench of smoke rolls over them. Strings of light pop in the branches of the Christmas tree as flames run up the yards of gold ribbon and ornaments shatter from the heat. The tree blazes like a sun.

The circle breaks and the revelers scatter into tables, chairs, each other, climbing over waiters and stepping on dress trains while the doorman approaches, indomitable as a siege tower. And then everything slows. Lacunae reveal themselves in a pattern, a path. He knows where to go. But first—

Henning swings his fist, sending the host careening into a plate of canapés. He clasps the baby tight against him as he runs through the gaps, dodges a screaming empusa, jumps over the shards of a serving bowl. The doorman's clawed hands reach for him, so close Henning can smell his breath—he jukes left, missing the giant's lunge, and does not look back when he hears the doorman hit the floor, trampled by the guests. He flees, down the steps and driveway and into the street where Connie's running the car, one arm waving out the window while the other leans on the horn. He dives into the passenger's side and fights to close the door as Connie peels out onto the highway.

◆

Only after he searches for an inhaler in the glove compartment and the vise on his lungs loosens and the baby stops crying can he take a true, deep breath. The dashboard clock reads 3:15; its cream-colored light reflects off the steel lighter Connie holds against the steering wheel. They drive in silence, listening only to Henning's hummed lullabies and the drone of the car as it flies up the Byway.

"I've been to better parties," Henning says.

"Shut up," Connie replies, eyes fixed to the road, "just let me think."

He cradles the sleeping child in his arms. "... You're heading north?"

"Yes. We can drop her off at the firehouse in Manchester and find a place to stay until I can negotiate a truce."

"You don't think they'll ask questions? Call the cops?"

"Then we'll leave her outside the door."

"She'll freeze to death!"

"It'll be a mercy compared to what Paulfry will do to her if he finds her! I've seen what happens!"

"It will be in every newspaper and on every broadcast by tomorrow morning and he'll know exactly where she is." He inspects the scratch on her cheek; it's already crusted over. The charms on her collar sparkle under the bloom of each streetlamp they pass. "Maybe we can take care of her for a while. I basically raised my sisters, I remember how to keep babies alive."

She slams on the brakes and a tight grip on the door is the only thing that stops him from slamming his head into the windshield. The baby whines and he rushes to calm her.

"What the hell is wrong with you," he starts to say, but stops as Connie's glare burns through him. Her teeth glimmer in the half light.

"I will toss that child into the sea if you suggest we keep her. I will eat her myself."

"I'm not saying—why are you being cruel?"

"Tell me something," Connie says, "are you prepared for the day she breaks a bone playing in the dark? For when she's lost and you can't search for her because it's the morning? When she opens the curtains at daybreak and maims you, when she splits open her thumb and you devour her? Could you bear that guilt? And if you're lucky enough not to have killed her before she's grown, could you watch her die of old age? Could you resist turning her?"

He hesitates. "So what if I did? You turned me. It could be the three of us."

"If you care for that girl at all, you wouldn't condemn her to the world that's coming. And you say I'm cruel."

The fury drains from Connie's face like a rush of blood. She sighs, then presses the gas pedal and drives on.

"We need to go. The day's almost here."

Beside the road and under the cliffs, the ocean stretches into the black horizon and heaves itself against the rocks, as if trying to scramble onto shore. In the quiet they can hear its howling.

They'll wait out the day in Manchester, Connie says, and then they'll rehome the child. Relatives, strangers, a childless fae, she didn't care. Henning nods; the baby slumbers. He tucks her head under his chin and breathes in her scent of newness, of baby powder and milk. He thinks of all they'll need as he cleans the blood off her cheek with a wet thumb. A cradle most definitely, bottles, diapers. New pajamas, perhaps a yellow raincoat. Toys. Books. He's too distracted by his list to notice that he sticks his thumb back in his mouth, until he tastes a vague metallic sweetness.

Snow falls thickly, insulating them in a darkness cut through only by their headlights, but even now the cloudy edge of the Atlantic turns a soft grey. Dawn approaches. The three travel north, outracing a star.

WARNING!

THIS FALL, DO **NOT** BUY THE **SHOCKING, ACTION-PACKED, MONSTER-FILLED** NEW GRAPHIC NOVEL CALLED

LET US PREY

if you are easily offended by:
- STRONG FEMALE LEADS
- SPLATTERPUNK GORE
- DIVERSE CHARACTERS
- AWESOME ARTWORK.

If the above does not offend:

GRAB THE ~ALL-NEW~ SPLATTER WESTERN GRAPHIC NOVEL FROM ARTIST ADAM JAMES & WRITER VICENTE FRANCISCO GARCIA FROM:

DEATH'S HEAD PRESS

DEATHSHEADPRESS.COM

SUSAN AND THE MOST POPULAR GIRL IN SCHOOL

JACK LOTHIAN

SUSAN slips into the restroom on the first floor. She should be in class, but sometimes she likes to hide out here, and sometimes—if she's lucky—the teachers don't notice. There is still another year of high school remaining, and she plans to ghost through it, as invisible as possible. She imagines her yearbook picture being out-of-focus, indistinct, fading year by year until it was like she was never there at all.

The far right cubicle is her preferred hiding spot—furthest from the door—but she stops short as she approaches it. The door is open, but someone is already there. The most popular girl in school is on her knees, retching into the bowl, shoulders heaving.

At first, Susan thinks the girl is probably purging, keeping off the weight, all the better to squeeze into those cheerleader outfits. But then the girl's back arches sharply. The noises change, becoming stranger, almost animalistic. The body shudders, and Susan sees what looks like black vomit pouring from the mouth, into the bowl below. She steps back, horrified.

In that instant, the most popular girl in school whips her head around, looking straight at Susan. The girl's eyes are a jaundiced yellow, and there is a smear of black around her lips. She springs to her feet. Susan keeps backing away, stammering an apology. The girl moves towards her, out of the cubicle, across the restroom floor, each step deliberate and precise. Susan backs up against the sink, and there's nowhere left to go.

The most popular girl stops, right in front of Susan. The girl's jaw is gently twitching, as if she's preparing to speak. She stares at Susan an unwelcome stain she's only just noticed. Susan averts her eyes, towards the tiled floor. She hates being looked at, and has never felt more seen than in this moment.

"I have to go to class," says Susan. "Please."

The most popular girl in school leans forward, and Susan flinches. But the girl merely moves Susan out of the way, and runs her mouth under the faucet. She gargles water, spits it out, thin rivulets of blood swirling down the drain. The most popular girl checks her reflection in the mirror, re-touches lip gloss, and then walks out, without ever acknowledging Susan's presence again.

Susan stands there, awkward and frozen. It takes a minute for her to catch her breath. There are jigsaw thoughts, almost forming in her head, but never quite fitting. Fragments of fear, brushing up against an odd sense of disappointment, now the moment has gone. It is as if she had witnessed something forbidden, and although she doesn't understand why, she knows she needs to see more.

◆

After classes Susan sneaks up onto the bleachers. She hides up at the back, in the shadows of the gym, and watches the more popular girl run through cheer drills with the others. They're all beautiful and perfect, a different species. They turn the music up, whooping and shrieking, as they power through their high energy routines. Even though the girls all follow the same steps, there is something primal about the way the most popular girl moves, something fierce and wild, that sets her apart from the rest.

Susan sees the quarterback, Bryce, jog over from the doorway. He whispers something into the ear of the most popular girl. The most popular girl laughs, but she doesn't smile. The quarterback and the popular girl have been dating for months. They will be crowned King and Queen of the Prom. They carry that easy sense of entitlement, where such things are pre-ordained and expected. They are effortless in their happiness, gliding through life in a way that Susan can't even begin to imagine.

That weekend there is a party down by the lake. Music, dancing, a keg. All the good-looking kids are there. The popular girl and the quarterback sneak off into the woods sometime before midnight and don't return. Susan hears about it all on school on Monday morning. People love to gossip about the popular clique. It fills the empty spaces, gives them some form of ownership over what is out of their reach.

Susan is at the water fountain, head down, pretending she hasn't heard the bell for third period. The corridor has emptied, everyone scattering for class. Susan looks over and sees the quarterback is still there, staring into his locker. He is pale and has dark circles under his eyes. The most popular girl approaches him, and he tries to smile at her, but it's clearly an effort.

When she reaches over to caress his cheek, he can't help recoil. That seems to please her, and she strokes the back of his head as he turns away, gazing back into the dark emptiness of the locker. The most popular girl whispers something to him, and then moves off down the corridor. As she reaches the junction, she spots Susan down the hallway, and she winks at her.

It feels like a small bomb going off, and Susan looks away, cheeks burning.

Susan is not used to being noticed. She is one of those people who has slipped through life's cracks. Never a part of the in-crowd but also didn't gel with those on the outside either. She wasn't particularly unpleasant or worthy of ridicule, just blandly inconspicuous, and those that did notice her never saw anything worth investigating further.

She had perfected the art of creating fake friends and events to keep her mother from worrying. Most weekends—if she isn't taking care of her little brother—she heads out to some fictional social gathering she's conjured up—*I'm going over to Lisa's house to watch movies, I'm shopping with Lisa and Kara, me and Toni are going to ride our bikes around the lake.*

There was no Lisa or Kara or Toni, but Susan could imagine their faces, their personalities, creating a whole inner life for herself as she traipsed aimlessly around malls and outlets, drifting for hours. There were sporadic moments of reflection in which she was acutely aware she was searching for something, even if she couldn't say exactly what that was.

That evening Susan tells her mother that she is off to the movies with the non-existent Kara. She cycles her bike through the twilight suburban streets, seeing how the quality of housing improves with every block. The lawns become crisper, the drives longer. It is only a few streets, but it might as well be a journey to a different world.

She stops outside 105 Ridgewood Avenue, and ditches her bike on the sidewalk. She hurries, keeping low, around the side of the house, skirting the fence that keeps the yard in. She's been here once before, a few years ago, when there was a pool party for the popular girl's birthday. Susan had 'accidentally' walked past a few times. At the time she still held some mistaken hope that one of her classmates would spot her, call her over, invite her into their world. But nobody noticed, and nobody called.

She doesn't know why she's here, just that there is some unknown force pulling her into place. She gazes up to the most popular girl's room. The shades are down, but the light is on. A silhouette flits by. Susan pictures the most popular girl, crossing the room, texting her friends, oblivious to the fact she's being watched. It feels like a strange sort of victory.

And then the silhouette freezes, dead center of the frame.

Susan holds her breath as if she's been spotted, even though she knows that is impossible. Then the dark outline raises both its arms and starts to move. It is like a dance, but the motion is jerky and flickered, like an old film clattering through the projector. Susan can't take her eyes off it. Even though she's hidden by the fence, separated by the yard, the glass, the shades, it is like they are in same the room, face to face, only now Susan is brave enough to meet the most popular girl's eye.

The arms twist and turn in impossible shapes, faster and faster. Susan can hear her heart beating in her ears. It is the crack of the snare drum, the thud of the bass, a primitive rhythm, a soundtrack to this dance, and it joins them together, faster and faster, about to burst into a crescendo when the room suddenly cuts to black.

Susan crouches there, muscles aching. A thin sliver of sweat trickles down her spine. She stares up at the black window for a long time, but the light doesn't come back on.

The show is over, if it ever was a show.

◆

The next morning at school, the loud-speaker summons the seniors to the assembly hall. The principal approaches the microphone, and in a hesitant and cracking voice, he informs them that yesterday evening Bryce, the quarterback, took his own life.

Ripples of shock spread across the room. Susan sees people starting to cry, a spontaneous reaction that sweeps down the rows. The most popular girl crumples, sobbing into the shoulder of a friend, shoulders heaving. It reminds Susan of the restroom, the retching over the toilet. Susan finds herself pushing through the lines, towards the most popular girl.

She is drawn to her. Metal to magnet. Moth to flame. She jostles her way past mourners until she reaches the most popular girl.

"I'm sorry," says Susan. "I'm sorry for your loss."

The most popular girl doesn't turn around. She is still crying, wrapped in the arms of a friend who is simultaneously comforting her while motioning

for Susan to go away. Susan doesn't want to go away. She wants some sort of acknowledgment. She is owed that much. She grabs the most popular girl by the shoulder, forcibly turning her.

"I said I'm sorry for your loss." Susan is aware she's almost shouting the words, but she knows the girl will understand.

Yet the most popular girl shows no sign of understanding, only tear-stained incomprehension. There is no flicker of recognition at all. Her friend pulls her back inwards, like a precious doll.

"What the fuck is your problem?" says the friend. "Leave her alone, freak."

People are staring at Susan. Even in the grief of the room, the opportunity for gossip, some minor scandal, is too good to pass up. Susan feels a crushing weight of unexpected humiliation. She had convinced herself that there was some secret bond between her and the most popular girl. Without realizing it, it had given her a sense of belonging, of purpose, and now that has been ripped away from her. Head down, she hurries for the exit doors, almost tripping up as she goes, hating every eye that's upon her.

Classes are canceled for the rest of the day. Susan roams the mall. She sits in the food court and nurses a flat coke. Her fries grow cold. Everything around her feels plastic and fake. She counts the days left of high school. The number seems impossibly high.

◆

Her mother greets her at the door, face sketched with worry. She places her hands on Susan's shoulders, leading her into the house.

"I heard about Bryce. I am so... so sorry." She strokes away a strand of hair from Susan's face.

"It's okay," says Susan. "I didn't really know him."

"You were at his birthday party last month," says her mother, more with concern than suspicion.

Susan remembers she had used that as an excuse one night. She told her mother she was heading to the party, but actually rode her bike out to the old quarry, wheels shaking across the gravel and dirt. She cycled around the edge, circuit after circuit, trying to lose herself in the mindless repetition.

She imagines Bryce at his party, surrounded by friends, posing for pictures, his big warm smile. Then in his room, alone, the final moments. A scared teenage boy, hands fashioning a tie into a noose, a storm howling in his head that he cannot hope to understand. She finds herself choking up, on the edge of unexpected tears.

Her mother pulls her close. "I know that it's not easy sometimes. But if you ever—if you ever feel that way... I'm always here for you, Susie. You're not alone."

"I don't have any friends," says Susan, relieved to finally say it out loud, to admit it to someone other than herself. "Nobody likes me. I just—I just can't fit in."

"That's not true," says her mother.

Susan looks up at her, nods, wiping away tears. "I'm sorry."

"Susan, you have friends. Really, you do."

Susan thinks she can hear a strident level of hope in her mother's voice as if by repeating it enough times, it will make it true. But her mother continues. "Like Lisa. She called around for you earlier. She's upstairs, still waiting in your room."

Susan turns and looks towards the staircase that rises into the dark. There is no 'Lisa'.

And Susan does not have any friends.

◆

The most popular girl is sitting on Susan's bed. As Susan opens the door, she has an inappropriate twang of shame over her room; the patterned Goodwill bedcovers, the poster of the boyish singer who is no longer in fashion, that pink stuffed unicorn on the shelf.

But mostly she feels a cold, quiet, fear.

The most popular girl rises from the bed, and then extends her arms and starts to twist them back. Susan can hear bones straining beneath the skin. She wants to shout for her mother, for help, but she can only stand there and watch.

"What are you?" she manages to whisper.

The most popular girl looks like some unknowable statue, an ancient carving, dug from a forgotten tomb. Arms bent and angled. Head raised, staring up towards an indescribable sky. Susan hears the crack of cartilage.

Then the girl jerks and twists back into shape. She steps towards Susan, all focus on her, and Susan feels the room shrink and contract around them.

"Stop watching me," says the girl, and she places her hand on Susan's wrist, as if to restrain her. "And stop following me around."

"No," says Susan, although she doesn't understand why she's refusing. She wants to ask what happened to the most popular girl, but she can't

find the words. It doesn't seem to matter, as her unasked question gets an answer anyway.

"She's sitting by the lake, watching the shadows grow. Above her the black stars blink into existence. Every moment lasts an hour, and every hour lasts a life time." The girl's voice is a low hiss, like steam escaping a rattling pipe. "Would you like to join her? Do you wish to see the nameless places, to kneel before the tattered hem?"

Susan shakes her head. The girl has gripped her wrist, a vice of iron. Her touch is far colder than Susan could have imagined. Her face is so close to Susan that it blocks out everything else in the room. "I'll eat your soul. And the soul of your little brother. Then your mother. Then your father."

"Good luck with that then," says Susan. "My father walked out years ago. Nobody knows where he is."

Susan isn't trying to be funny, but the most popular girl seems to smile at that, head tilted, maybe even amused by the response. Except the smile keeps growing, the mouth gapes open, and the jaw starts to unhinge and click, and Susan desperately tries to push the girl away, which only seems to galvanize her even more. Susan stumbles back against her bedroom wall, closing her eyes, turning away as the girl moves closer. She imagines the jaw extending, the darkness inside spilling out and swarming over her, jagged teeth tearing at her flesh. She reaches out a hand to stop the imagined attack, but it swats at the empty air. She opens her eyes. The girl has gone, and she is alone again.

Outside the neighbor's dog starts barking, and doesn't stop all night.

A few years ago Susan found a large envelope of letters, ripped and torn up, hidden in the back of her mother's closet. She recognized her father's handwriting. She managed to piece the scraps together, a painstaking task, hour upon hour. She expected to read words of sorrow and regret, pleas to see his children. But there was only a stream of bile, aimed towards her mother, saying how much he despised her, how she'd ruined his life. Susan and her brother never even got so much as a cursory mention. The hole her father had left transformed into an echoing void.

◆

The next day at school Susan eats alone.

Out the corner of her eye, she sees the most popular girl putting food on her tray, ignoring the line. Susan will not look at her. She has made a decision. There is still a year to go, and she must be invisible again.

The most popular girl approaches her and stands for a moment, before placing the tray on the table. She sits down in the empty seat opposite from Susan.

The rest of the school looks on, unsure what to make of this unprecedented social juxtaposition.

The most popular girl takes her juice box off the tray, punctures it with a straw.

"Do you want to know my real name?" she asks.

"Not really," says Susan, eyes down, focusing on her food.

"We were there at the start. When man crawled from the slime, and gazed up into the cosmos, it was our unblinking eye that stared back down."

The girl is trying to sound triumphant, but to Susan she just sounds tired, as if she's going through the motions.

"I don't know why you're still here," says Susan. "It's like you're stuck and can't go home or something."

The girl says nothing for a moment, then she leans forward, pushing her tray to the side. Her voice is low, a purring growl.

"I meant what I said last night. I could eat your soul."

Susan shrugs. "Yeah. I heard you."

The most popular girl shakes her head. "You must be really desperate for friends."

Susan looks up at her. "You're the one that sat down with me."

The most popular girl in school appears to consider this. Then she nods, as if it makes as much sense as anything.

The two of them sit there, eating in silence, as the rest of the world carries on around them.

IN THE WAR, THE WALL

SASWATI CHATTERJEE

"How old were you when the War began?" asked the doctor. He sat with his back to his guest, sunlight illuminating a tired face with a greying mustache. It was a sweltering day, and he had abandoned his slate grey coat on the back of his chair, choosing instead to open the windows and let the occasional breeze in.

The man opposite him had made no such concession; he was dressed in a cream-colored suit and the humidity in the air didn't seem to bother him as much as his host. His black hair was brushed back neatly; on his lap was a pale felt hat. He tilted his head at the question.

"I? In 1914, I was a boy of eighteen; the terror of my nurses and the despair of my parents." He smiled briefly. "That was after I met him, of course."

The doctor smiled at the mention of their mutual friend. They were seated in his chambers in Cornwallis Street, Calcutta on a sultry summer afternoon. Outside, the city moved along sluggishly; the occasional cry of a passing hawker pierced the sleepy silence.

There was a soft knock and the doctor looked up as a woman pushed the door open.

"*Jol khaben?*" With a glance, she noted his guest and quickly pulled the end of her long sari over her head.

"My sister, Beena," the doctor said. His guest got to his feet and bowed deeply. "This is Mr. Hayashi, who has come from Japan."

"Oh!" Beena said, blushing faintly. "Please don't mind me, I will bring some tea." Her English was lightly accented.

Before Mr. Hayashi could say a word, she disappeared around the door. The doctor laughed.

"She is shy, don't mind her."

"Not at all," Mr. Hayashi said, sitting down. He put his hat aside and sat straight-backed on the cane chair provided. "You are not married?"

"No." The doctor replied. "Before the war, I might have, but now the desire has quite left me. And Beena is a willful thing, don't let her behaviour fool you. I have my hands full managing her."

Mr. Hayashi acknowledged the remark with a smile. He said, "I am sorry to have come to you about this so suddenly, Doctor Bose."

"I was startled when I got your telegram." The doctor said. "Even more startled to find that you knew him. I haven't heard anyone mention Mehroor Khan in years."

"I knew him for a short while in Japan." Mr. Hayashi said. "He grew to be a dear friend. I always wondered what became of him and…"

"I am sorry that I was the bearer of such news."

"No, I had the feeling it could be so." Mr. Hayashi paused, seemingly lost in thought. "He was a remarkable boy. Man." He shook his head. "I'm sorry, it's been so long since I've seen him that I can barely think of him as the man he must have become."

"You met him in your childhood?"

"When I was fifteen, yes. His father came to Yokohama on business." Mr. Hayashi smiled briefly. "He was the first outsider I had seen. I preferred to keep to my books, but my father insisted I eat dinner with them, and that is how we met." He chuckled. "He was so very quiet in the beginning."

"Knowing what I know of Khan, I cannot imagine he was ever quiet."

"Haha, yes. He was shy at first. His father did most of the talking. I was sent to show him around the house—the elders had to discuss business, you see. I showed him the gardens and we spoke a while. It was… difficult, in the beginning. He spoke English fluently and I, not as well. But he was very interested in everything I showed him, from the flowers to the *shishi-odoshi*. Oh, how he was fascinated with it. I still remember him rushing back to his father afterwards to demand that they get something similar for their home." Mr. Hayashi shook his head. "What a talking to he got. But they were with us for five days after that and in that time, we grew quite close. He was a great talker and I loved to listen whenever he spoke. I had never met someone like him before. Someone quite so—"

"Charismatic?" The doctor was smiling. Mr. Hayashi tipped his head in assent.

"Yes. And when he left, I was despondent for days. My father promised me he would take me on his next trip to India. But the war dashed those hopes."

"Among many others."

"Yes." Mr. Hayashi paused for a moment before asking, "His funeral was well attended?"

"I am sorry to say I did not go. It... it was a difficult affair." The doctor drummed his fingers on his desk. "I haven't been in contact with him for many years."

"Why is that?"

The doctor hesitated. "Are you a man for strange stories, Hayashi-san?"

◆

Beena showed them to an inner lounge and served them tea, disappearing as quickly as she had come. Mr. Hayashi sipped the sweet, milky tea as the doctor took off his glasses and placed them on the table in front of him. In the dim light, he looked older than he was. Older, and very tired.

"There were six of us," he began. "This was in Ypres, Belgium. There were two *sipahis*, Thapa and Mann; two civilians; I, a sub-assistant surgeon at the time; and of course, Khan."

"He was Subedar-Major in those days—the highest rank granted to Indian soldiers. I think we thought it was a great thing at the time." He laughed dryly. "If only we knew... Poor boys. Poor boys, us all. We never knew what we were getting into."

"Few seldom do, where wars are concerned." Mr. Hayashi said.

"The war was bad enough. It was this *other* business..." He stopped and shook his head. "I'm going about this all wrong. Best to, as they say, start at the beginning." He took a sip of his tea.

"You asked me why I didn't go to the funeral. I'll tell you why. They are mourning a man I barely know."

The doctor looked up.

"Let me explain.

"Very few remember Khan as he was. Those who do are either dead, or old like me. He was a different man when I met him. Not... *better*, you understand me? Just *different*. More decisive but also more impulsive. Not entirely a bad thing, but you must remember that we were in the middle of a war.

"But it won him a great many friends, I among them. He was well-regarded even among the white officers. I often heard our commanding officer say that if he wasn't brown-skinned, he would have risen through the ranks. The sipahis in the regiment liked him too; he was companionable, told jokes even at the worst of times, and stood by you. In the war, you needed a friend like that. God knows I did.

"We were part of an Indian regiment sent to France; we landed in Marseilles before being sent to Belgium. Along the way, we became fast friends. His family and mine were of the same social class, and we found that we had much to talk about. He told us all kinds of stories about travelling the world, including, yes, going to Japan, and the strange and wonderful things he saw there.

"Half the time I didn't know whether to believe him! But those were strange times, when a man wanted to believe in strange things. Besides, the men and I would have believed him if he said he had spoken with ghosts.

"So when Khan told us we were to shelter in the old church, we followed, as we always had."

◆

"The war was nothing like we had expected. We had been in skirmishes back home, but this was a different beast. We hid in trenches all day; those who went over were cut to ribbons. I grew to dread the smell of sweat coming from the men next to me—the rank smell of terror and exhaustion mixed with urine and death.

"Khan remained calm through it all, but it was a near thing. I don't remember much of my time there, but what I remember very clearly is his reassuring hand on my shoulder, with the *rat-tat-tat* of machine guns above us.

"In those days, I was sure I would die there—across the water, in the white man's land. Men were dying like flies around us. But somehow, we survived. Until that day.

◆

"We were on retreat. I could hear the firing above us, behind us, around us. When the bombing began, the dead began to proliferate. I remember sprinting back through the remains of the city, trying desperately to read signs in a language I barely recognized. But it was impossible. Nothing was as it had been even a few hours ago. The city had been reduced to rubble and ash. Everywhere I ran, there was a body underfoot. I was a man trying to pick his way through a graveyard.

"In the midst of this, I found Khan. There were two other sipahis with him, poor souls like me. I remember I laughed when I saw him—*he's alive, he's alive!*—and he took me by the arm and shouted:

"'*Chalo, doctor!*'

"We fled from street to street, with only a vague idea of where we were going. It was difficult to find our way amidst smoke and shouting and screaming. I remember seeing several dead horses and pitying the poor things, brought here to die in an alien world. The ground was muddy; our boots sank in and we struggled to pull them out. I would not say we ran so much as floundered. Periodically, a great cloud of mud and debris would blow up somewhere close to us. I did not pay any great mind to this. I just kept moving.

"When I later learned how much of the city had been lost in the artillery fire, it sounded unbelievable. That complete devastation, the loss of an entire city... and yet I had been there. And, well, the things I have seen since... .

"My apologies, where was I? Ah yes, the Germans were bombing and we were running, just running. I don't remember having a clear plan in mind, other than just following Khan. Somehow, even in the madness, I found that I had the willpower to trust him.

"Somewhere along the way, we had picked up two civilians. They were injured when we found them, and doubtless would have died. I told Khan... but never mind, I have told you this.

"We moved again after we found them, slowed down, but now the bombing was behind us rather than around us. I began to feel hope when Thapa, who had run ahead, shouted to us that he had found an intact building.

"It was a church, and miraculously, it appeared to have escaped the worst of the shelling. Many years later it occurred to me that this alone should have struck us as strange.

"Barely a building around it was intact. Yet it did not seem strange for us to follow Khan in there.

"This church, how do I describe it to you? I feel like I must, even though it was nothing remarkable. From the outside, the building itself wasn't much different from churches here in Calcutta. It had a tall spire, the end of which had been knocked down. The front doors were heavy wooden double doors, painted red, under a stone arch. As we got closer, I could see that it was damaged; the wall to the right had caved in, and the doorway was piled high with rubble.

"Inside, the pews had been smashed to bits, and pieces of once-beautiful stained glass windows lay shattered on the floor. I remember stepping on the glass and wondering which saint's face I was stepping on. It almost felt blasphemous.

"Hayashi-san, I will tell you this: even now, when I close my eyes and think of the war, I think of this place first. Not the bombs. Not the bullets. Not the thousands of men abandoned among the ruins. But that narrow rubble-strewn path. Dust everywhere and us choking, dragging the civilians along. And that room... that room, Hayashi-san, how do I tell you about that room? It *haunts* me.

◆

"It was the work of a few minutes, removing the rubble near the door. The civilians were in no condition to help themselves so it was the four of us who got them through the door. Thapa carried the woman in, half fainting. Her daughter was mostly awake, one half of her pale face blood-splattered, as I hoisted her in my arms and carried her inside the airless church.

"I say airless, because that is what it felt like. From the moment I entered, my breath was taut in my lungs. Thapa nearly staggered and Mann had to rush and grab him. I thought the boy would faint, his face was so pale. But somehow, between the four of us, we managed it, and I ordered them to lay the civilians down on the ground and began to check my supplies. Truth be told, I felt a little dizzy as well—whether from blood loss or the intensity of the last few hours, I didn't know.

"All this while the sounds of bombing had retreated to a shallow buzz in the distance, as if we were leagues away from the action rather than just a few streets. I remember wondering at the lack of sound, but I was also grateful for it and paid it little heed. I had two patients to tend to, after all.

"The next few hours, I remember very little of. Some memories do come to mind: Khan pacing, always pacing. Mann sitting across from me, watching me tend to the civilians. Thapa, pacing as well—he would get as far as the door, glance out and then resume.

"None of us left.

"It might seem, Hayashi-san, by my descriptions that we were waiting for something. And we were. But for what, I never knew. My breath was razor sharp in my lungs. I felt like if I said a word, it would cut my throat.

"By late afternoon, my head was beginning to feel heavy. I remember leaning against a wall and then suddenly sitting up again because the wall felt wet. *Spongy.* At the time, I put it down to combat fatigue, but the dreadful *wetness* of it... I can still sometimes feel it trickling down my ear. It's enough to drive a man mad, I tell you. And we *were* being driven mad: by the war, by the suffocating silence and by the *tap-tap-tap* of Khan's pacing.

"It was near evening when the distant sounds of the shelling finally stopped and I told Khan that neither of the women was going to live. I ought to have told him that before, but I... could not. It seems almost nothing now—two people we would never meet again—but in that moment, it was devastating.

"Who were they? Ah, I forget their faces. A mother and her daughter, I believe. Yes, dreadful, isn't it? Dreadful how I've forgotten their faces. At the time, I swore I would never.

"I remember the ghastly expression Khan had on his face when I told him. I remember because it looked a lot like *hope*, except run wretched by the war. I knew what he was thinking: now we could move faster, without their deaths on our conscience. We had tried. *He* had tried.

"I imagine much the same thoughts were visible on my face as well.

"But then his face changed and he glanced at Mann and Thapa, both dozing beside the dying bodies, and said in a low voice, 'Come see this, Doctor. I've found something.'

"He led me behind the altar and to the unassuming looking door I had taken to be the priest's quarters. When he opened it however, it led to a dark staircase. We both peered into it.

"'Cellars?' I asked him. He shook his head.

"'I've heard they have tunnels down there.' He struck a match, which barely lit the entrance. 'We could look around, avoid the streets.'

"I was dubious. This was not how I had hoped to leave. I remember arguing with him fiercely in

whispers.... The bombing seemed to have stopped, in the dark the four of us could make our way out—

"He laughed in the face of all my arguments, but acceded to one point. He would go down and take a look. If it seemed like a dead end, we'd abandon it. How did that sound to me?

"It sounded terrible. But I could find no position from which to push back against that disarming smile. He was so eloquent in those days, Hayashi-san. I was like a moth to his flame. I had no chance.

"I let him go.

"We waited. After a while, Thapa awoke and asked after him. I pointed to the door and told him what had happened. He went up to it and looked down and I saw him turn pale. Thinking something dreadful, I rushed to the door and looked down, but saw nothing. Turning to Thapa, I demanded to know what the devil he had been playing at, scaring a man like that.

"'Very sorry, sir,' Thapa told me, 'but the smell is horrible.' He turned away from the door and, stumbling to the altar, proceeded to empty the contents of his stomach in a splattering mess on the floor.

"Only then did the smell hit me. Sour, like Thapa's vomit, and pungent like the piss and sweat of dying men, carried through air laden with heat and death—like a trench stuffed with corpses.

"I sat with Thapa after that and took his pulse. He shook in my arms as I did it. His pulse was weak, but recovering. I lay him down, with stern instructions to rest unless he wanted to keel over. From the corner of my eye, I caught a glimpse of Mann, watching us with feverish eyes. Another dying man. Two dying men, and a third at the bottom of the stairs.

"What would you have done, Hayashi-san?

"I'll tell you what I did. I went down the stairs.

"It was a short descent and soon I was at the bottom, peering into the endless darkness. It smelled pungent and the walls were wet with some residue. I put my nose to it. There was no smell, which was an odd thing in itself, considering the sheer number of other odours that were assaulting my senses.

"I lit a match and found myself looking at the opening of a dark tunnel. I stepped forward, and immediately my match flickered in some wind I could not feel. I stopped and listened as hard as I could—there was nothing. I promise you, there was *no sound*.

"I waited for a minute or two but soon that terrible darkness began to feel like it might suffocate me. I steeled myself; if I didn't go now, I would flee screaming from this place. And I began to walk.

"As I recall it now, it felt like I walked for hours, but the sipahis later told me that I was down there no longer than fifteen minutes.

"My remembrance of this is unremarkable. That's funny, now that I think about it. The rest of my memories are alive with the sharp stillness of that day—the church, Khan, the men—but this walk, this long walk, I almost remember it with fondness.

"The tunnel turned twice and then ended abruptly. I was almost at the end when I knew I wasn't going to find Khan. I stood at the last bend, where I could just barely make out the dead end a few yards ahead of me. The lit match I was holding was burning down, and my matchbox was almost empty. I blew out the one I was holding, struck another and began to turn. Even then you see, I was thinking that perhaps I had missed a turn somewhere behind me.

"In that darkness, I heard a sound. I will remember it till the day I die, but I don't know how to describe it to you. Choking? Yes, that's right. I stood in the darkness and heard a man choking to death behind me.

"I turned.

"He was there. Or rather... no, no, he was there. It was him. Him in that wall. Him with his arm stretched out towards me, half-embedded in the *wall that was eating him*.

"Forgive me for that pause. You are very attentive, Hayashi-san. I've not had such an attentive listener for a while. I will continue in a moment.

"He was in the wall. At first I thought, *he is stuck in a crack*. But then I saw the wall contract and relax, like a breath, and Khan's body slid in deeper. I saw one half of his face disappear into it. The remaining half—the remaining *eye*—fixed onto me with some sort of desperate intensity. His one dangling arm flopped helplessly like a fish. Half his mouth opened sluggishly and then closed again. I heard him choke.

"No, I heard him speak. He spoke. He said—
"'*Bhago.*'
"Run.

"How do I explain to you what I felt in that moment? I was not afraid. I was *awash*. I was teetering on the brink of a precipice. I was a child looking down into the chasm of my creator's mind, *and it had no purpose for me*.

"Are you a religious man, Hayashi-san? I was.

"The wall next to me was breathing. I could feel warm, wet, damp, *hot* breath washing over me, like that of a large dog. But this was larger than any dog. And quieter too.

"I remember looking at it and watching the bricks move. The wall breathed like a newborn foal, with jittery breaths, uncertain of what it was doing. Unclear of this new world, desirous of its purpose, just beginning to kick its legs—

"I give you the foal imagery, because it is the easiest. It is also completely *wrong*. I need you to understand this, Hayashi-san. It is wrong. It was nothing like a newborn foal. Only I, in that moment, cresting that mountain of madness, thought that it was, and that thought has stuck with me since then.

"If I had to describe it now, it would be like... a wall breathing. Exactly as ludicrous and terrible as that sounds.

"I did not run. I ought to have. But my legs, in a moment of supreme cowardice, would not carry me. I also found myself possessed by an incredible idea: I wanted to *touch the wall*. I wanted to see if I could feel the breath, trace the veins, find the beating heart.

"And in that moment, from the darkness, I heard the half-choked word again.

"'*Bhago.*'

"What do you think it takes to destroy a man? Death? Mutilation? Seeing the terrible toll a war may extract from a human body and yet not stop? The war should have been enough to destroy us all. That we lived is one of the only two pieces of evidence I have of the existence of a human spirit. The other is the man who tried to save me that night.

"Hayashi-san, you would be glad to hear this of your friend: All the love and humanity lacking in the war, I found that night in one man. My friend who loved me and asked me to run.

"I wish I could tell you I did something wonderful for him in return.

◆

"Where was I? Yes. I ran to the wall. At that moment, I had some half-baked notion of getting him out of there. I would not leave him to die. I did not realize that he was beyond death.

"My arms went around his waist, half of which was in the wall. I felt them brush against the insides of the wall, against the *Wet* and the *Sodden*. I am a doctor. I know blood vessels. And as I pulled, I heard them tear and watched as a stream of black-red sludge began to leak from the wall.

"Khan was weeping. At least, it sounded like weeping. But you could not have separated me from him if you tried. I had found purpose, and by the gods who had forsaken me, I was going to see it through.

"I tore him from the wall. Yes, *tore*. His head came last; I saw the wall *stretch* with his skin, and then I wrenched it free. As I did, I saw his eye, staring at the wall, at the insides of it. It looked forlorn. His other eye was fixed on me. It was empty.

"You see, Hayashi-san, here I arrive at the crux of the problem: It was me. It was *me*.

◆

"He was never the same, of course. I half carried him out of there and, when I reached the stairs, found Thapa and Mann making their way down. With their help, we hoisted him out and into the main room of the church. I remember telling them some dreadful made up story of foul smelling gases that would make a man faint. The Germans had been employing chemical gases, so I suppose it was not completely unbelievable. But, to be honest, I don't think I was very convincing. Yet they

saw my face that day and said nothing, and I could not have been more grateful.

"I won't bore you with the details after this: we found another regiment a few streets away and managed to get to safety. Mann died later that year—a grenade blew off his leg—and Thapa was part of the regiment sent to Egypt. I lost track of him. I believe he died there. As for me, I was eventually sent back to India when the war ended. There I found Khan again.

"I wondered, for years after, what would have happened if I had just… left him there. It's a dreadful thought, and not one any God-fearing man ought to have, but… now it seems to have been the only decent thing to do. The *right* thing to do.

"As for the rest of the story, you know what happened after, of course. He married a nurse he met at the hospital, and retired a few years after. He was decorated for his valor in the war, of course, and then he just… faded.

"I saw him on a few occasions, and he could not be more different than the man I remembered. He would begin to say something and then slip into a sort of puzzled silence. As if the words were there, but just beyond him. Or as if he had too many words, and none of them quite fit. As if he was quite beyond, as they say, the *human condition*. They began to say he was a bit touched in the head.

"We never met face to face again. It was my cowardice, more than anything. I was afraid of what he would say, though my strongest feeling is that he wouldn't actually remember me. But more than that, I was afraid of what he would *see*. If I was the catalyst that was needed to awaken something both mundane and yet dreadful—

—like a wall that breathed."

◆

The doctor stopped talking. Mr. Hayashi noticed that he was gripping the table very hard, so that his knuckles had gone white. In a moment most unlike himself, he put his own hand on top of the doctor's. He felt the man start.

"You were very brave, doctor." Mr. Hayashi said gruffly.

The doctor looked at him. "You loved him," he said, as a way of understanding. Mr. Hayashi wiped his eyes.

"A little too much. I told him I would wait for him. When he didn't return, I thought…"

"…that he wasn't coming back." the doctor finished.

"Yes. I married. She died a few years ago. And I thought I ought to come here. To see him and if he… remembered."

"I am sorry."

"No." Mr. Hayashi was smiling. "I am not sorry. I know my friend was loved."

"It is very generous of you to say so." He looked down at Mr. Hayashi's hand, which was still in his. Mr. Hayashi noticed, and with an apology, made to withdraw it.

"No, please." the doctor put another on top of his. "*Please*. You have been so kind to me. I ought to have died in that wretched place. You have—"

"You ought not to have, at all." Mr. Hayashi said firmly. He squeezed the hand once more before Dr. Bose relinquished it. In the dim light of the setting sun from the window, for a moment, Mr. Hayashi saw a much younger man—a man who would have run into the mouth of a horror to save a friend he loved. It made him miss the bright young man he knew, with an ache he barely recognized. He got to his feet.

"I have kept you for long enough. But I feel like I must thank you for this tale. But I…" he stumbled with the words. "I do not know how to."

The doctor also rose. He indicated the door behind him. "I know a wonderful little place for dinner. Would you like to join me?"

Mr. Hayashi hesitated, and then picked up his hat. As he turned, he paused for a moment to look at his now-friend.

"You were wonderfully brave." And then, with a lurch of pain somewhere deep in his being. "And how desperately he must have suffered."

"How desperately we all suffer." the doctor said quietly. "But yet, despite it all, here we are."

Mr. Hayashi smiled and took his arm.

THALIA WAS ALONE

DONYAE COLES

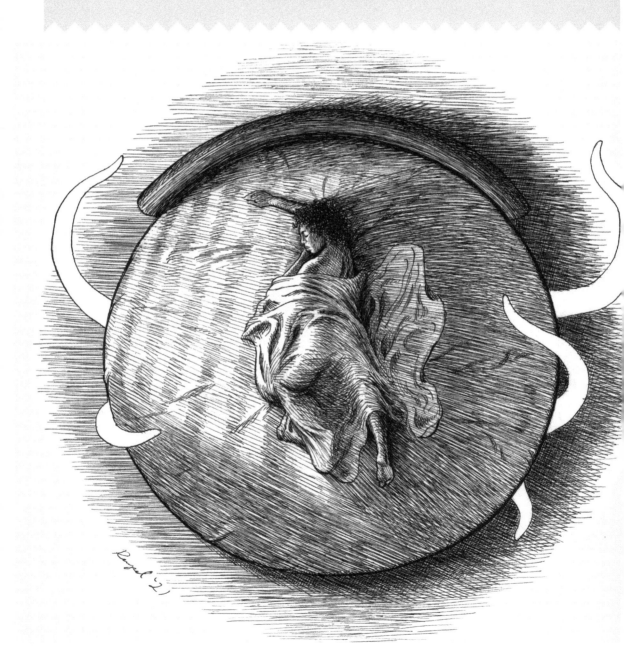

THIS is where it started. A rumor.

"It'll be cool," the Boyfriend said. He wasn't really her boyfriend but that's what she called them, the boys who came over and in. They didn't stay, of course. Thalia wasn't that type of girl. Thalia wanted everyone to love her, she wanted people to look at her and need to be near her. She put on makeup as soon as she woke up, rarely in the morning, and then cried for a few minutes so it would run and she would look more like Marla from *Fight Club* even though she was brown sugar sweet skinned and looked nothing like Helena Bonham Carter. Still, she had hollows in her collarbones and she looked hungry, not for food, but for something else. It was all right. She knew that about herself too.

This Boyfriend, forgotten be his name with all the rest, had that certain look in his eye when he told her about the party. The hungry, wet look that told her what he really wanted, what would be really cool.

And maybe Thalia wanted it too. It was so hard to tell what she did and didn't want when the Boyfriend told her what he wanted. And he wanted to get fucked up and swim in the sea of bodies, press himself into strange and watch strange press into her and that sounded good, that sounded fine to her. That's what the rumors said would happen, how it would be.

The rumors were true, most rumors are. There were bottles. There were pills. Bright red ones that went down like candy. Thalia floated on a cloud as they, the other party goers, caressed and stroked. Hands, mouths, everywhere. Pulling at her, needing her. All under the softest blue light. She wanted to take the feeling in, drag it into herself from between her legs and open mouth, swallow it until the pit of her filled to bursting.

All night, kitten touches, thick tongues, strong fingers until the twilight light turned black and the pieces of her shattered into tiny specks of dust and she was gone, gone, gone.

Morning came. The Boyfriend was gone, really gone. The hands were gone. The mouths were gone. And Thalia was alone, wrapped in a worn blanket on top of a round bed, a castoff from some love hotel. That first day she found clothes, not hers but wearable. A baggy men's shirt and a pair of latex shorts that rode up her ass. Beat up jelly sandals half a size too big. She wandered through the house in her borrowed wardrobe, running her hands over the crown molding, the dusty furniture. The prints of other hands and other bodies

left behind by people who had exited before the sun rose.

A small house, a two-story, single family home deep in a rundown part of a city that had moved on. Empty lots sat on both sides of it, the neighboring homes long since torn down and the world was quiet. The house seemed in good shape to her. The floors didn't creak when she walked, the walls were white, not water stained. Good enough according to her two eyes.

She made her way into the kitchen and opened cabinets full of food with labels she didn't recognize. They were almost right, but they weren't any off-brand she had heard of. Spaghet-spheres, Ripping Chips, Peppy Cola. The only thing in the refrigerator was a glass bottle that held slightly blue milk. She sniffed it, determined it smelled alright, made herself a bowl of Cap'n Crux and ate it at the chipped kitchen table.

She ate alone, no one came down or in. Just her and her knock off cereal. Thalia noticed in that strange animal part of her that lived in the back of everyone's head, she didn't feel alone. The animal part of the brain was never wrong at least she hadn't thought so before then because she saw nothing with her own two eyes, there was only that feeling and that wasn't enough. Finished, she put her bowl and spoon in the sink. If she had thought about it, she would have noted, later, that the bowl and spoon were gone when she had lunch. But she was used to being cared for and she didn't think about it.

She swept the house, searching for what weighed on her that felt so much like someone else in the empty building. A tired couch in the living room that faced a white wall. Up the stairs, a second bedroom that held a tired twin bed covered in a worn blanket. She tripped back down finding an empty coat closet and inside that a second door but when she pulled on the knob it stayed shut, keeping her out. She closed the door and thought nothing else of it. Thalia wasn't the type to dwell.

The first day she sat on the couch and played on her phone which never seemed to die. She drank the bluish milk, ate the off brand food. She fell asleep in the love motel bed, buried under worn blankets. Blue light wrapped her dreams tight, and she sighed and sang in her sleep as it touched and teased her, like so many fingers, so many hands. But it was just the one blue light. She woke up happy but alone still. She repeated the process on the second day and night. On the third she left the house on Everton and returned to her apartment.

Her roommate poked her head out of her own room. "Rent's due," the woman said eyeing her slowly before asking, "You ok? You look different."

"I'm not wearing makeup," she mumbled in return, slipping into her room, shutting the door. A mattress shoved onto the floor, a pile of clothes sitting on the floor with it. She shoved the clothes in boxes, the shoes in a suitcase. Her makeup back in the bag. She called a cab and started walking her things back down the steps.

"You still owe rent!" her roommate yelled as she took the last bag down the steps. Thalia didn't respond. Forty minutes later, she gave the last of her money to the driver and climbed out of the car at the house. The door swung open and it felt, when she stepped past the threshold, that the world sighed.

"I'm back," she said to no one at all and took her boxes and bags up to the room with the love hotel bed.

No matter how she felt though, she was alone, anyone with eyes could see that and Thalia did not like to be alone. The house on Everton was lonely and she was alone and that just wouldn't abide.

She started a rumor. A text message to someone that could almost be called a friend, a few comments that dripped of unsaid promises that were just waiting to be filled in. Gold poured into the cracks of her rumor as they spread, making them shine with imagined possibilities for people like her. The people who didn't like to be alone but were so, so lonely.

She slept and waking found the house filled with bodies, bottles passed carelessly between them, red pills traveling from fingers to lips. Smiling she joined the fray.

She danced and howled until stumbling she went to her room to find the press of bodies, the soft blue light that had held her that first night, then release and deep, content darkness. In the morning, no matter how good and soft she had been, she woke alone. Just her and the house. She drank the milk, ate the food, stared at her phone until the time came and she started another rumor.

A stream of Boyfriends and Girlfriends and none of them touched what she dreamed that blue light, soft as anything, could be if it just kept stretching, filling, reaching. But still she wanted them, needed them. Needed to not be alone.

In its emptiness the house hummed and vibrated. *It's trying,* she thought in the empty hall. Thought it strange but thought it anyway. The water came from the faucet the perfect temperature when she wanted a bath. Just the right things were in freezer, in the cabinets when she was hungry. A blanket just in reach when she felt cold. But she was alone and that she couldn't stand.

"You're different," her friends who weren't her friends commented on her latest photo. "We never see you out anymore."

Her skin was clear and taut, she glowed. Her hair, usually a dry bush was thick and full, the tight curls springy to pull on. Her eyes were bright and big in her face. Everything about her looked full and she wanted to dive in and swim in herself. She didn't look like Marla from *Fight Club*. She looked like something darker and fiercer and she liked it. Liked the look of herself. "I don't go out anymore, come to my next party," she wrote back.

She wanted to bring them all to the house. Wanted them to share the love hotel bed. All the little faces on the phone screen. She dreamed her bed stretched beyond space and they all crawled inside of it, everyone that ever was and they all loved her in the way she wanted to be loved.

She fell asleep daydreaming on the couch and felt the ripple of fingers against her in her deep dreams. She woke to a knock on the door and the world covered blue in twilight.

She stood, pulling on her sleeves, staring at the door curiously. There had never been a knock on the door. Slowly she opened it and he stood there, smiling, showing off teeth that needed a dentist but didn't make her shy away. Something about him held her, door open, waiting.

"I heard," he said slowly, "that there's supposed to be a party here."

She nodded and stepped back, letting him pass, no reason to stop him. He had come on the tails of her rumor. He had come because she called but he didn't look like anything that she had called. He looked like something that had blown in from the desert, all dry and hard. Nothing like the soft souls of the city that usually filled the house, nothing like her.

He stalked through the rooms, sniffing, and she followed meekly.

"This your house?" he asked slowly, opening the fridge.

"No, I just stay here," she answered, fighting the urge to close the door, push him out.

"They let you?" he asked, a lilt of surprise in desert wind.

"Nobody's said anything yet," she mumbled, unsettled.

He nodded and shut the door, turning and smiling widely at her. "That's just perfect then. Just fine."

The press of his lips felt like sand on her, his every touch on her skin felt like sand pressing against her. His hands under her shirt, the knee that pressed between her thighs. There and solid but not. Like he would cover her, press all the air from her lungs, replace it with himself. "Take me upstairs, I'm your new boyfriend."

She found, as soon as the words spilled from his lips, dusty and as dry as her mouth after his kiss, that he wasn't wrong and that going upstairs to the round bed and all its worn blankets was exactly what she wanted to do.

Different and new, that animal part of her recognized something dangerous about him. Something that was off in her world but she couldn't stop, she marched up the steps, his heat following and showed him right into the bedroom she slept in.

"Nice tits," he said when she slipped off her top. She laid under him, the world heavy but the color all wrong, not the blue, no, something more like gold.

It's fine, she told herself her eyes fluttering closed under that strange golden press of him, the way he seemed to sink into the cracks of her, dry and wrong. *He'll be gone in the morning. He's not like the others though, maybe he'll stay.* She didn't know if she wanted that or not. She couldn't tell, with the Boyfriend, her thoughts felt fuzzy. Just like all the others before him.

She found him tangled in the blankets when she woke again. She wasn't alone.

She slipped out of the bed and found more bodies. Their breath heavy in sleep, slumped against the wall, strung over the couch. *The party,* she reasoned, brushing her curls back. *People stayed.* The animal part of her brain growled and

bucked sending electric ice down her back that twisted her guts but she ignored it, pushing it away because he had stayed. They had stayed. The air felt dry.

Thalia was not alone. And even as that animal part of her screamed that she had missed something important, she didn't care. She could see, with her own two eyes, that she had exactly what she wanted.

She hummed and went to the cabinets to find them full, as always. She opened the fridge to find the milk, still cold but slightly yellow. She sniffed and wrinkled her nose. The milk had gone off.

He didn't leave and neither did they. Not that day, not the next. Or the one after that. More people came. They filed into the house and stayed, covering the floors and she held a frantic court. They sang her praises, they did mad dances to be close to her. The walls turned greasy with their touch, the air smelled of waste. He sat on the couch, her king blown in with the wind that finally, finally stayed, and she sat next to him. They drank, they swallowed pills, little yellow ones now, and it took her days and days to realize that it was not a party.

When he went to bed, she went to bed, and when she woke, they were all still there, cluttering the floors. The cabinets emptied, the garbage and dishes piled up, the milk spoiled.

Thalia's hair fell out, long strands shed all over the floor. Her hips and breast lost their fullness. Her eyes sunk into the sockets. Her makeup ran and she looked like Marla again, better than before since the brown sugar sweetness of her skin paled and faded. If the Boyfriend noticed, he didn't say anything. He just fucked her and showed her to his friends. It was fine. This was what she wanted. To not be alone.

She found the door in the closet, the one she had forgotten about, all splintered and broken a month after he had come. A heavy wet scent wafted up from it. "There's a leak. I'll fix it," the Boyfriend told her without asking, dragged her up and away from it. Kissed her too hard and she didn't think anymore of it. Later, when she saw the open door again, the air that came through was hot and dry like a fever.

No one ever left. The Boyfriend that felt like the desert, like the sun, never left. His friends never left but Thalia felt alone. She missed the blue press and the kitten-tongued girls and boys of her parties. She missed the quiet press of the house. She missed the warm, wet blue of her dreams that didn't come anymore in the dry too hot space of what the house had become. She stood in the living room, staring at the bodies draped all over, the once white wall all dirty with their prints. Her eyes settled on the Boyfriend. A king in his court.

She made a choice.

She turned, marching back up to the room that held the round bed and he followed. He always followed as if he had to be stuck to her in the house, couldn't be away from her. He scratched his bare chest and sat on the bed.

"You're destroying my house and I want you to leave." The words tumbled out of her mouth and the animal part of her knew they were exactly the truth. Howled with the rightness of it.

He chuckled. "This isn't your house, honey. Come here, I'm feeling a little dry."

She shook her head. "This is my house and I don't want you here. I don't want any of you here!"

He looked at her strangely. She had never said no. Could never say no. She wasn't that type of girl. She hadn't been.

The house shifted.

Like an earthquake but instead of moving the furniture, all of reality stepped slightly to the left and now she saw what was and wasn't the house on Everton. What had always been a house and had never not even once been a house. The world turned blue.

The bed split under the Boyfriend, showing sharp lines of teeth for a moment before they came crashing down on him. In two chomps he was gone, his little blood red pills on her face. The thing that had been the bed lifted and twisted itself before Thalia in its full glory.

She stared at its fat, luminous body, a part of its total being. She understood in that animal part of her that the blue of the world was the thing before her, that the thing before her was this world. Around her the house collapsed, the sound of

wood and plaster restructuring itself came from just beyond the door. There were people screaming. All the sounds that she had dreamed through, wrapped in blankets that weren't blankets, enveloped in the blue of the house. The flesh of the house. The house that was this thing.

It shuddered and the light changed, the blue turning more gold for a moment and then a sick seaweed color, mottled and off. What it had swallowed was not something it could survive. But it had, for her. Because she wanted the Boyfriend gone and it had made it so.

But she understood then that it had let the Boyfriend stay. To make her happy. Because she did not want to be alone.

Because it did not want to be alone either and if the Boyfriend stayed, she would to.

It had no limbs, only short, pucker-less, tentacles that lined its body, hiding the part of it that had swallowed the Boyfriend. It looked like jelly, glistening and wet.

It inched towards her, holding out its tentacles, searching, needing.

The animal part of her reacted before she could and she reached back. *It'll be alright,* she would have said if it had not happened so quickly. One blue tentacle wrapped itself around her arm and it, the house, pulled her in.

The blue surrounded her, she floated as those short tentacles probed her, searching for something. This is what she wanted. It pulled gently at her skin, before finding entry into her. As she floated in it, it pushed into her. Its tentacles slipped inside, past both sets of her lips reaching towards the center. The animal part of her hummed, only pleasure, endless pleasure and that feeling. That thing she had wanted more than anything at all.

And it could not survive, not after what it had done, not without her. And she pulsed need and desire in return.

Oh yes, they thought, together as one, *I'm not alone.*

Thalia woke up slowly inside of herself, breathing contently in the parts of her that were empty. She had become they and they were full. They dug out Thalia's phone from the nest of blankets and started a rumor.

They were full, yes.

And together. Not alone.

They meant to stay that way.

OUT OF THE DARKNESS

JENN ASHWORTH
EUGEN BACON
SIMON BESTWICK
GEORGINA BRUCE
GARY BUDDEN
MALCOLM DEVLIN
RICHARD V. HIRST
VERITY HOLLOWAY
TIM MAJOR
LAURA MAURO
ALISON MOORE
GARETH E. REES
NICHOLAS ROYLE
ASHLEY STOKES
SAM THOMPSON
ANNA VAUGHT
ALIYA WHITELEY

OUT OF THE DARKNESS
EDITED BY **DAN COXON**

OUT OF THE DARKNESS
Edited by Dan Coxon,
Shirley Jackson Award nominee

Featuring stories by Alison Moore, Aliya Whiteley, Georgina Bruce, Simon Bestwick, and Laura Mauro.

All royalties and editor's fees from this collection are being donated to the mental health charity Together for Mental Wellbeing.

SEPTEMBER 2021

ASHLEY STOKES

"It's not often these days that I laugh out loud when reading a book, but this one is rich with brilliant comic moments. Loved it."
GARETH E. REES,
author of
Unofficial Britain and
Car Park Life

GIGANTIC

GIGANTIC
Ashley Stokes

"Unlike anything I've read before. Absurd and inventive, *Gigantic* made me laugh and shake my head in equal measure."
Lucie McKnight Hardy, author of *Water Shall Refuse Them*

"Loved it."
Gareth E Rees, author of *Unofficial Britain*

SEPTEMBER 2021

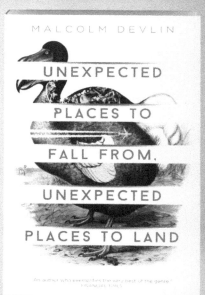

MALCOLM DEVLIN

UNEXPECTED
PLACES TO
FALL FROM,
UNEXPECTED
PLACES TO LAND

UNEXPECTED PLACES TO FALL FROM, UNEXPECTED PLACES TO LAND
Malcolm Devlin

"Stories like this are exactly why I love to read."
Nathan Ballingrud
on *You Will Grow Into Them*

"Malcolm Devlin is one of our finest voices."
Angela Slatter

OCTOBER 2021

UNSUNG STORIES

nsungstories.co.uk

Rempel '21

ONLY MY SKIN THAT CRAWLED AWAY

THERESA DELUCCI

THEY'D been driving around the desert for the exact number of days it took Gena to skip to a different song on Jessie's playlist without asking.

It was a decent run though, going that long without getting on each other's nerves. Gena had only tolerated some twangy, sleepy folk-rock because Jessie wanted a lonesome cowgirl vibe on her big birthday trip, but Joshua Tree on a Tuesday in the shoulder season turned out to already be the most melancholy place in America. In early December the days were short and cold enough that any *Thelma & Louise* antics were sealed up like the roof of the silver convertible Gena had optimistically rented and there was no shirtless Brad Pitt on the side of Route 62, just strewn trash and boarded-up buildings that Jessie remembered being vintage shops three summers ago.

But the sky above the park was still the widest Jessie had ever seen, especially this past year, and the clouds hung back enough so that they could see all the way from the Keys' View lookout to the blue shimmer line of the Salton Sea. She loved showing Gena the desert for the first time, dropping names for what they saw along the hiking trail into the conversation like dollops of whipped cream; *quail, mariposa, creosote, jackalope*.

Gena kept stopping every few feet to take pictures. They had an earnest but noncommittal intention to "make art" on this girls' trip, but had instead shuttled through the week touring Palm Springs' dispensaries and plugging the new, awkward silences in their conversation with silly stop-gap debates about why *American Horror Story* sucked this season and which married men they knew and would absolutely fuck were they more mercenary, including their own (but never each other's) husbands.

Gena invented a game where they had to switch sunglasses and tell each other what they saw through the other's eyes. That sounded plausibly creative enough to keep Jessie from hiking too far ahead. Her pair of scuffed drugstore throwaways turned everything "whiskey-gold," Gena said, like the dead end of a summer day. Gena's polarized shades remade the world in blues and pops of crimson bursting from chuparosa bushes and, to her surprise, open veins of quartz in the boulders. They reminded her of the bloody strokes she'd made up on her own inner forearms, with a crueler brush.

Jessie peeked under her sleeves to see what color her scars might be now, six months After—always a little mental capitalization when she thought of time in those private epochs. Looking with Gena's eyes, through Gena's shades, Jessie thought her scars looked like fat, red sea worms, but Gena probably would've described something more gracious. Because that's how Gena saw the world and Jessie could not.

"Feels like I'm at the bottom of the ocean," Jessie said, pulling the sunglasses off.

The faces on the missing posters at the visitor center were never far from Jessie's mind. There were backpackers who hadn't been seen since July. Jessie absentmindedly erased her own footprints in the dirt with sweeps of her boot while Gena took out her camera again.

If their remains were ever found, weeks later, desiccated as cholla skeletons and clinging to one another in some pitiful sculpture, the final photo in the camera's roll would be a record of their feet standing on the ground at the precise moment both women, unbeknownst to the other, realized that their long friendship might well be over when they returned to New York.

◆

They hiked another two miles before Jessie decided they had gone far enough. The sun was lower than the mountains and it was only three o'clock. Tracks went in all directions between the scrubby brush; not all of them were human. A thick blanket of clouds unrolled from the east and if it rained, even those breadcrumbs would wash away.

It was only an out-and-back trail, but neither woman fully trusted they were going the right way until they saw the parking lot. It was much closer than their fear (and dispensary purchases) made it seem. They laughed as they got into the car, agreeing that their epic trek surely earned a drink before they checked into the AirBnB. Gena's hardcore whatever-it-was battered through the stereo without remark from Jessie.

A gust of cold wind buffeted them through the doors of the only saloon in town open for a proper happy hour. In Jessie's Western movie, she and Gena were mysterious and alluring gunslingers, not two women on the wrong side of thirty-five and obviously not locals, dressed all in black and faces brightened with makeup even for a day hike.

It was dark inside, until their eyes adjusted to the glow of Christmas lights draped over the barback mirror. Greasy smoke poured off the barbeque pit out back, crispy at the edges with the bite of fresh-cut limes. Jessie hung back a few paces and watched every man perched on a barstool track Gena's hips as she followed their waitress past a display case of souvenir T-shirts to a table in the center of the room. They turned their heads in unison, all wore the same oily jeans and heavy Carhartt jackets, and Jessie thought of Tippi Hedren walking past a murder of crows on a playground.

Far away from home, sipping from sweating mason jars of margaritas, and rolling her eyes at horny losers in Gena's wake, everything felt familiar again. Like this wasn't the first time Jessie had really hung out solo with Gena since Jessie's last impromptu getaway, which also involved a lot of talking about men and making art. Only all of Jessie's drugs were prescribed and she was on an involuntary hold.

Tequila made Jessie swagger as much as leering men goaded Gena into performance. Gena insisted they have another round, so it was the perfect cocktail for Jessie to play-act her seduction tactics on one particularly inappropriate crush. Loose-limbed, Jessie got up and stood behind Gena, and so laced her hands in Gena's perfect curls to tilt her head back.

Gena smoldered on command, her dark eyes narrowed and glinting above her grin. Jessie just sucked on Gena's lower lip, rough, like how she'd kiss if she were a cowboy, until the tip of Gena's tongue nudged into her mouth.

"Hey, now." Jessie laughed it off with warming cheeks.

Their floorshow was definitely noticed by the huddle of men at the bar; a big guy with a fat face as red as his hat howled and someone else whistled. Too many faces crowded the mirror behind the shelves of booze. The same expression of mean hunger smeared over their eyes as they looked at Gena, only Gena, and their reflections moved too slow when they lifted their arms to take long pulls from their beers, like the men were trapped under the greasy glass.

All of Jessie's big cowgirl energy blew away like a tumbleweed. Even Gena picked up on the sudden shift in mood and asked for the check. The sun was down and Jessie dreaded what the twisting dirt roads would be like in the dark almost as much as having to walk by the men again to leave.

From the heated passenger seat of the car, Jessie watched Fat Face stroll out of the saloon and light a cigarette. He leaned against his mud-died truck and she kept watching him watching them before Gena peeled out of the parking lot and he retreated in the side mirror.

They were speeding through the black, knowing that the darkness behind them meant no creeps were tailing the car, when Gena slammed on the brakes with a "shitshitSHIT!" and threw her arm over Jessie's chest. Barely ten feet from the bumper was a padlocked gate and tiny white PRIVATE ROAD sign.

"I think this is it," Jessie said, scrolling for the starred email from their host on her phone, holding it up to find a stronger signal. "Yup. Got the combination."

Gena looked at her expectantly.

"Yeah, yeah, I'm going," Jessie said, grimacing even before she got out of the car.

Gena pulled the door shut behind her.

"Gee, thanks." She pulled her hood up and trotted to the gate. She grabbed the thick, cold chain until she found the rusted lock, hefting it with one hand and trying to line up all the numbers while directing her phone's flashlight in the other. Her freezing fingers felt too big and before she could thumb to the final number, she fumbled her phone and it bounced out of sight.

She crouched and felt around. Gena was obscured behind the windshield. If a night could gather, this one was a thick blanket bunched the wrong way, alive and waiting for her to retreat before it unfolds again. Close, too close, Jessie heard twigs snap. She was suddenly aware of how puny the headlight beams were, how small she was in them.

Gena flicked on the brights and Jessie jumped. She snatched up her phone and finished entering the combination, relieved when the lock pulled apart and she could swing the gate open.

Jessie jogged back to the car and flung herself into the passenger seat.

"Aren't you going to lock it behind us?"

"House rules don't say we have to." Jessie took one last look into the dark before she pulled the door shut so hard it made the window rattle. "And what if we need to leave in a hurry?"

Gena frowned. "It could be keeping things *out*, you know."

"I'm freezing," Jessie said, and that was her final answer.

◆

Gravel crunched under their tires on the careful drive down the street. The cabin was supposed to be on five acres of desert, but the listing didn't mention that the land was in the dead center of a small valley—like a crater on the moon or a blast site—ringed on all sides by houses on the surrounding foothills. Jessie wondered how much rain it would take to pound it into the mud, hoping the storm that threatened them all day kept away.

A second combination to a lockbox and a finicky housekey later, and they were inside. Even accounting as Jessie did for an acceptable margin of wide-angle chicanery, the place was small and "rustic," it turned out, was a euphemism for worn. The living room anchored the L-shape of the cabin, a narrow hallway led to the bedrooms and bath. The exposed wooden beams of the ceiling that had looked so earthy and warm in the online listing absorbed the light, drew the eyes down to the flimsy furniture and flat white walls. Crammed in the far corner was an open galley kitchen with scuffed green tiles set in dirty grout.

"At least the heat works," Gena said.

"Ah, so that's what that noise is." The air vents shook with a bass-heavy hum Jessie likened to the Brown Note, that precise low frequency noise police pumped over loudspeakers for riot control. She felt the thrumming in her sinuses and teeth, not her bowels, yet, thankfully. They couldn't find the thermostat.

"You're like my husband. Just tune it out."

Jessie tried. Every time she stopped acknowledging the sound, the heating system would kick back on with a soft *thunk* that sounded like a car door shutting outside and echoing around the valley. Even better, it made this noise at irregular intervals; Jessie'd be taking her best stab at mindful meditation as Gena poked around the kitchen cabinets, then, *thunk*, "Oh hey, the Manson Family's just pulled up in the driveway!"

They wouldn't see anyone outside if they were really there, because there were no blinds on any of the windows in the whole house and, like the drive up to such an imminent crime scene, it was pitch fucking black outside. But anyone could see *them* inside, in the light, just fine. Jessie shielded her eyes and pressed her face against the window across from the sofa to peer at a lone Joshua tree in the front yard. Its spike-fisted branches were flung up into the night. She tried not to imagine the red laser sight of a sniper rifle dotting her chest.

Gena called her husband, but Jessie used her last burst of energy to take a shower. The water got about as hot as she expected and, despite the listing's promised amenities, there was no soap or shampoo, so she mostly just spread the trail dust all over her skin in a gritty film.

The house felt a hundred degrees too warm; Jessie pulled on the one tank top she had packed. She brushed her teeth over the sink, examining the faint sunburn on her neck. Her arms were still pale but for the long threads of scars up her forearms, puckered and pink, but less angry than they were even a month ago. She was getting used to this new skin. It was a part of After, too.

Jessie walked back into the living room to see Gena pulling a long face by the front door. Her stomach sank.

"What now?"

"Oh, I don't wanna say..."

"Just tell me. A roach? A *scorpion*? C'mon, Ripley, we can handle a bug hunt."

"The deadbolt doesn't lock."

"Well, fuck." They tried pulling and lifting the door as best they could, but it was misaligned vertically because of course whoever took care of this dump didn't give a shit that the house was sinking, like everything else in this town.

But the host made sure desert-themed dioramas littered every tabletop—ubiquitous succulents, palo santo sticks in ceramic bowls, rusted candelabra. A dusty stack of country records leaned against the living room wall with no player in sight. That's when Jessie realized the house wasn't really meant to be slept in at all; it was just a place for pink-haired Instagram models in floppy hats and ponchos to have their pictures taken as they clutched tin mugs of coffee and stared off into Coachella sunsets. #Grateful.

Jessie flopped onto the sagging futon before noticing the giant stain in the middle of it. Maybe the house was a backdrop for other kinds of pictures. The stain became even more suspect. She scooted closer to Gena to avoid it.

"At least it's not blood."

Gena put her arm around Jessie's shoulders and squeezed. "I'm sorry. I wanted this to be more fun."

Jessie caught Gena trying not to gawp at her arms, so she turned her palms out to give a better look. Jessie shrugged. "I've stayed in worse places, right?"

Gena winced.

"Scars are sexy. May I?" She put two fingers to Jessie's left wrist, like she was testing for a pulse, started to trace the scar higher, higher.

She flinched. "I didn't do it for the 'gram.'"

"I know." Gena put her other arm around Jessie and hugged her so long it had the opposite effect of comfort. In the window across from the sofa, their reflections looked close as ever, but Jessie's arms wore the proof that it wasn't true. When Jessie pulled away, her hair was pasted to her neck. Gena thumbed fat tears from her eyes that could have been for any number of things Jessie didn't have the heart to say out loud tonight.

It was too late to drive back to Palm Springs, un-floppy hats clutched in hands, because they weren't cut out for even the tiniest bit of roughing it. Gena suggested they sleep in shifts, which seemed extreme, but Jessie was probably only going to toss and turn anyway, so she volunteered for first watch.

The bedroom Jessie claimed had a floor lamp with a red, fringed shade, an odd-man-out amid the phony desert nomad chic. It cast a scarlet light into the room, part bordello, part slaughterhouse. She kind of liked it. It wasn't the best light for actually seeing anything, but she busied herself laying out clothes for the morning anyway, the faster to flee at dawn. She hummed a tune she had just invented called "Leaving Murder Cabin (#Blessed.)" The thought of returning to a heated hotel pool lifted her spirits as much as her evening dose of meds.

Gena padded into the room wearing only a T-shirt and boy-shorts.

"Can I sleep in your bed?" She sounded more timid than tempting, but Jessie still rolled her eyes.

"We're *so* getting murdered tonight."

"We're too old to be mistaken for co-eds. We're probably safe," Gena said.

She tucked herself under the covers before Jessie could say no. She didn't know what Gena was playing at, if she was going to try for another hug, or a big discussion, or if Gena was just afraid to leave Jessie unsupervised. Gena fell asleep before she could find out.

Annoyed, Jessie took her cellphone to the living room.

She opened a window in the kitchen to let out some hot air and smoothed a blanket over the futon before sitting down. She sat in the dark, texting her husband most of the days' events knowing that it was too late for him to reply. Something made her not tell him about the kiss. He wouldn't be mad, because he only really got furious at her the one time, for what she had done to herself. She plain hated to admit that he was right though; she wasn't ready to travel yet. But she had insisted. They both needed a break from his nurse duty.

If she were to try explaining to him, she'd say that Gena only knew one way to show love, but she didn't want to be so cynical. Jessie was like the damaged nerves she could sometimes feel reknitting under the skin of her wrists, making her fingertips burn; love was the phantom limb of her feelings.

Jessie put the phone down and leaned back on the sofa, staring ahead through the wide front window. The lights of other houses dotted the hills, other lives as far from hers as stars. It would be easy to open the broken door and put one foot in front of the other to reach them across the empty dark. Jessie listened for the next *thunk* of the heating system to measure out time.

She stared until the lights in the distance blinked out one by one.

◆

She didn't know what time the light in the bedroom came back on or if she had instead opened her eyes, but she knew it was the sound of a car door shutting outside that roused her from the dark hole of thoughts. The reflection of the hallway behind the sofa glowed lurid in the window and Jessie looked over her shoulder, trying to see if Gena had gone back to her own bed or if her shadow moved under the bathroom door.

The house stood still, more solid than it had ever looked in the light.

Jessie faced the window again. She could barely see her own reflection hunched on the sofa. She tried to listen for what was outside, under the pressure building up around her eyes, making her molars thrum in their sockets. The red, reflected hallway ended in darkness, too, blacker than the light years between stars and all the tiny joys of living. From that fanged shadow, a long, dark leg stepped forward and the rest of Gena emerged.

It took a breath's time for her to register that Gena was naked. Cold uncoiled in Jessie's gut. Gena's bare feet slapped against the floorboards as she shuffled down the hall. The wild black brambles of her hair hid her eyes but her mouth shaped Jessie's name out of wounded animal noises and in that keening was the plea between them for Jessie to decide what must happen to them now. Yet Jessie's reflection in the window remained frozen on the sofa and when she felt the weight of Gena's hand gripping her shoulder, she didn't trust herself enough to push it away or pull Gena down closer to cover her up.

Clear as her own breath, the soft sound of drip, drip, drip fell steady on the carpet. She sat transfixed by that mirror-Gena in the window, with forearms black and slick as eels in the burning light and Jessie understood how far Gena would go to make them both the same again, right down to the topography of Jessie's own skin.

It might feel like an act of love, if only Jessie's burning fingertips could reach it from the right angle.

"It's not the same," Jessie said but all that came out was hitching sobs.

In the valley, all manner of animal chased each other between the larrea, their barks ricocheted off the rocks and careened back into the house through the open window in the kitchen. Her eyes were hot and wet, but she saw the murky faces surface behind the smooth windowpane like expectant sharks, and they began to jeer and howl at Gena's back in the way Jessie had only known so many men to do, with desire and demands.

She turned to look behind her and her breath seized in her chest.

Gena was not in the room, but Jessie didn't think for a second that she was alone.

They don't see me, she thought. *They never see me.* It had been all she ever wanted, once. Perhaps she could still run right past them. She could run in any direction and even Gena would not see her anymore, if she ever saw her, knew her, at all, even now, or if Jessie was just as much of a reflection for Gena.

Please don't see me, Jessie wished, before the heat and the barking and the smell of roasted meat became too much for the walls to bear and she felt the cabin shudder that much deeper into the earth and the front door bowed open with a resigned creak.

Please don't see me.

◆

When Jessie slipped into bed next to Gena, only dawn could be seen through the windows, a safe, pale orange line above the foothills. Gena rolled over to face her, eyes half-closed and gummy with sleep.

"You weren't here when I woke up," she mewled.

Gena sat up and hugged her knees to her chest, pulling the white comforter up to her neck. She looked imperious as a queen sitting in a row of hieroglyphs. A pillow mark gouged her perfect cheek.

"I got up to look for you."

"You did?"

"Uh huh. First, I looked in the other bedroom. But the bed was still made. So I went to check the living room." She spoke without looking at Jessie, her voice faraway in remembering. "Then, I heard the saddest noise I ever heard. I was so afraid of what could make a noise like that."

"Like what," Jessie asked, not wanting to know.

"It was so pitiful," Gena's voice became higher, like she was trying to mimic it, but mock it, too, and Jessie's stomach turned to ice. "The saddest little noise, like a mouse caught in a trap that just won't die on its own. And then I realized what it was."

"Stop it," Jessie said, shivering deeper into the sheets.

"It was *you*. You were *crying*."

Jessie's fingertips began to tingle.

"I made myself go into the living room even though I was so scared of what I might find." Gena paused and swiped an errant hair from her eyes. "You wanna know what I found?"

She shook her head, *no*, but her whole body was shaking and Gena wasn't looking at her anyway.

"Nothing. The front door was open and you were gone." Gena did look at her then, full-on. "You promised you wouldn't do that to me again."

No, Jessie thought and sat up in bed. "No, no. I was here the whole time," she sputtered.

"It's like I don't even know you anymore," Gena said.

The biggest accusation of all, the one they'd been dancing around all week, and before that, ever since Jessie carved those dividing lines into her arms; up and down the highway, and Jessie sped in one direction and Gena went the other, but never asked why. No tidy explanations in After.

Jessie rubbed and rubbed her bare arms but couldn't get warm.

Her arms, now smooth as glass.

Jessie stared at Gena in stunned silence, the beautiful face was the same, more familiar than her own for all the time Jessie admired it, but the eyes were not the eyes she recognized. It wasn't the color, exactly, but the cold shade of difference between Gena being afraid that Jessie was gone and Gena being scared that she was left alone.

"Give them back, give them back," Jessie shrieked, suddenly, clawing the comforter away from Gena's neck. "Who are you?"

Gena twisted away and swung her feet off the bed. Jessie launched at her back as Gena fled the room.

"They were mine. They were mine," Jessie screamed behind her the whole length of the hallway, making deer antlers and sage bundles and rose quartz rain down from the upended table by the door, until she caught the back of Gena's T-shirt and wrestled her to the floor of the living room. "Let me keep this one thing that's *mine*!"

"I didn't do anything," Gena repeated and repeated as she kicked away and grabbed for the broken doorknob, as if saying it enough could convince them both that she felt no trace of guilt about anything, ever. "I didn't *do* anything!"

Jessie yanked on the arms of the woman who was no longer her friend and flipped them over.

"Then why are you wearing my scars?"

Outside the open front door, Jesse saw all of the paths she might have taken away from this moment. The tracks were laid out before her in all directions, not all of them human. One set of footprints broke away from the rest to disappear beyond a solitary Joshua tree, whose shadow, she learned, neither lengthened nor constricted upon the demolished earth.

CODE WHITE

J.R. McCONVEY

Hᴇ knew the boiler room would be unlocked just as surely as he'd known, from his first day on the job, that something was living inside.

He was sitting in a brightly lit meeting room when he noticed the Breath. It hit him like a stomach cramp; a sudden, panicked awareness of the gargantuan noise coming from the ducts, roaring into every corner of the room, carrying the slight sweetness of decay. His dozen or so new colleagues, dressed in escalating tiers of Banana Republic office chic and collectively staring into the grille of a black conference phone, didn't seem fazed. Beth, Lydia, Adelaide, Jeff; Beth, Lydia, Adelaide, Jeff: Jakub assigned to each of them one of the four names he knew belonged to someone in the group. They were acolytes in a sacred ring, leaning in to listen to the Director, Karyn, speaking over the line.

"'The best way to find yourself,'" she said in a crackly voice, "is to lose yourself in the service of others'... That's Gandhi. Metrics show he beats The Dalai Lama for inspirational almost four to one."

"Better clickthrough," said a Jeff, nodding and tapping at his phone.

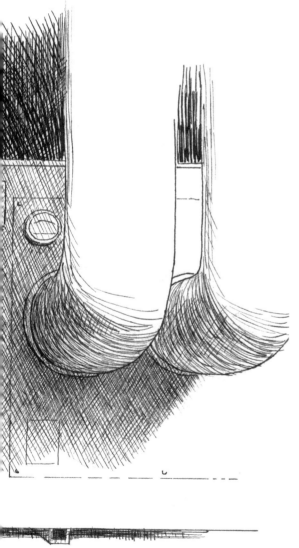

Jakub had gone through six interviews to get this job in the Strategy and Communications department of the Bethel-Day Health Centre. He thought about what his father would say, frowning out from under his impeccably trimmed grey moustache, if he knew that, on Jakub's first day, in his first meeting, when he should have been alert and professional—grateful for steady work, in these times—Jakub was distracted to near panic by the deafening bellows of the Breath filling the office suites of the Health Centre's Executive-Admin building, so huge as to become the air.

Am I crazy? he thought. *Can no one else hear this?*

For the rest of the meeting, he sat fiddling with a loose button on his green gingham shirt, feeling the heat of hives starting to colour his chest, acutely aware of a Lydia who'd noticed him daubing beads of sweat from his temple.

◆

Curiosity got the better of him, is what he told himself. That it was of his own volition that he ended up, a week and a half later, at the door of the boiler room on the first subfloor, ear pressed to the cold metal, listening. That he couldn't be sure it was unlocked, even though he'd already turned the knob, twisted it all the way to termination.

He stood, holding it like that, feeling the low vibration in the metal. Just a push, now. Slight pressure. Walk right in. See what's breathing.

There was still time for him to turn around. Leave it alone.

Avoid a Code of uncertain proportions.

Code Blue: Cardiac Arrest/Medical Emergency. Life hangs in the balance between death and salvation. The email, however, is rote, automated. A flat statement of circumstance, of which dozens of

Ramsel '21

identical versions flood Jakub's inbox every day, along with their rainbow of variations, the colours of disaster that bleed from the health centre's white walls.

Code Yellow: Missing Person. A patient disappeared, wandered off into the halls or out to the parking garage. Jakub's cubicle-mate, a sprightly blond woman named Kelly, told him there'd been a jumper the week before he started, off the P6 railing right across from the EA Building's fifth floor window.

"Like a flying squirrel," she said. "The way his gown spread out around him."

Kelly tosses stories like this over her shoulder while Jakub sits, deleting hundreds of Code emails between bouts of clicking out numbers on his keyboard. For the most part, the Codes don't affect him. He's here to crunch data, to predict the extent of the winter surge two years hence. His work will affect how the hospital treats people who are not yet sick, but who will be; his data guarantees their illness.

After four years of dealing at the casino to fund his statistics degree, Jakub isn't sure if it's fair to say it's paid off. He could do a lot worse than the Strategy department at BDHC. Some of his friends are still wiping down tables at the Pickle Barrel.

Code Grey: System Failure/External Air Contamination.

As a side hustle, Kelly runs a YouTube channel that has 90,000 subscribers.

Code Green: Evacuate.

Because he'd known the Breathing Man was there, because his Breath was ubiquitous, his presence in the boiler room did not surprise Jakub. In a room that was colder and clammier than the sterile hallways, a huge man-shaped figure crouched by the Air Handling Unit, pale as a parsnip, eyes closed, red-rimmed lips pursed up against the grille, breathing the steady, crushing sound that filtered up through the entire building.

At first, Jakub just stood and watched. The door eased shut behind him, leaving him alone with the Breathing Man. He thought he hadn't been noticed, until the Breathing Man's lips sucked together into a seal, cutting off his flow, and his eyes popped open to reveal huge pupils that shone with a glassy, opalescent light. He turned jerkily toward Jakub and opened his mouth to speak, but instead of words there came a brutalized rasp, like dusty cloth bandages being shredded to ribbons.

Jakub swung between disgust, pity, terror, and a hovering unreality that placed him behind his body,

observing their encounter from someplace safe, where it was inconceivable for such things to happen. The Breathing Man again tried to speak, but the same sound hissed out. Then, like a hurt animal—a great hairless goat, thought Jakub, or an enormous white grub, writhing in salty air—the Breathing Man twitched and cowered back, his body wracked with a spasm. Acid churned in Jakub's guts. He was no hero; just a numbers guy, more machine than man. Somehow, realizing this caused a surge of irrational bravery that moved him to speak:

"What are you?"

The Breathing Man swallowed and sighed. He turned to face Jakub, adjusting his crouch, wedging himself deeper beneath the Air Handling Unit he'd usurped.

"Ghud," said the man, and blinked. It was no word, but a strangled grunt, as though the man was gagging on his name. Jakub heard 'God' and almost laughed; this creature was too real, too present in the room, to be a manifestation of pure belief.

The Breathing Man turned and pursed his lips and pressed them against the grille, unleashing a sudden hiss of sour air. The sound of Breath again filled the cavity of Jakub's chest, blanketed the ceiling of his skull.

"What do you want from me?" said Jakub, voice thick with dread.

Only Breath answered, steady and consuming.

◆

Later, inside the Centre, Jakub walked the yellowed halls of D-wing. This section had purple wayfinding decals; he stepped on every one he passed, making his way along the path he took daily at lunch, a wending loop that only ever took him back to his desk. D-wing, which housed the ER and the critical and urgent care units, was over capacity. Beds lined the hall, housing the withered and elderly wrapped in sheets, plastic tubes running from their noises and needle-spiked forearms.

He turned a corner into the newer G-wing, whose upper floors were home to the palliative and ortho units. Here on the main floor, a bright windowed corridor led down to the clinical library and the auditorium where, next week, they would Gather Round—perform the monthly ritual of receiving the latest BDHC news from its dashing CEO, Deborah Merchant. Gather Round, Gather Round with Deb. Jakub imagined the Breathing Man siphoning huge gulps from the ducts of the auditorium, savouring the blended life-force of a hundred loyal employees in corporate rapture, rolling it around his tongue to try and find the strong, bitter tang of Deb Merchant's faith-borne exhalations as she emphasized for the hundredth time that they were *In It for Life*™.

Winter sunlight spilled in along the corridor, reflecting off the polished concrete floor. Down the hall, a man in a motorized wheelchair sat looking out the window, gazing at the grassy slope beside the parking lot and the fringe of trees visible beyond. Jakub had seen him here before, during his daily walks or on event days. Today, the corridor was empty, quiet. Jakub went over and stood beside the man, who turned his head slightly, then looked back outside, smiling.

"Beautiful day," he said.

The winter sun cast a silver haze over the trees. In the distance, a crow flapped in to perch on top of a dark spruce. Jakub studied the man's grey hair and the lines around the corners of his eyes and mouth, which seemed a diagram of confusion at what had become of him.

"It's nice to see the sun," said Jakub. He offered the man his hand. "Jakub."

The man smiled. He reached his left hand over, grasped the wrist of his right, and lifted it to place in Jakub's.

"Amir," he said. He glanced down at his hand. "ALS."

Jakub didn't know whether to squeeze the man's hand or not, whether he'd feel it. He gave the lightest clasp, for comfort or sympathy. Not that it would matter: this man's brain was losing the ability to control his muscles, his body slowly paralyzing itself. He was the colour and shape of sadness; yet he defied it by placing himself before the sun, breathing in light for as long as his ravaged neurons would allow.

"You're here often," Jakub said.

"Yes," said Amir. "I like talking to people. When you get sick, some of the people you know... they stop. Coming to visit. It makes them uncomfortable. To see how I've changed. Know what's coming. Even my wife. She tries to come every day. But it's too much for her." He waved his good hand through the air in a rough circle. "Now, the nurses. They're my family. This is home."

Jakub nodded. Amir sighed.

"First, you want more time," he said. "But time becomes a prison. Then, you wish for another body. Another self."

"I'm sorry," said Jakub.

Amir smiled again.

"Why?" he said. "You're here, now. Listening. It can mean a lot of things—to care."

The crow was gone. Jakub had to get back to his desk. Lunch was almost over and he hadn't eaten.

"There's a man in the boiler room," he said, staring out the window. "Sucking the life from everyone."

Amir nodded slowly, savoring the movement, his head almost floating.

"That's one way to look at it," he said.

◆

Code Purple: Hostage Situation. Code Pink: Cardiac Arrest/Medical Emergency – Infant or Child. Code Aqua: Flood.

Delete. Delete. Delete.

"I heard that last week," said Kelly behind him, "some nurse rolled a guy outside so he could die in the open air. Think about that."

Jakub fought the growing sense that he had always been at work and always would be—that he no longer left the office at night, but simply went dormant, hunched at his desk, breathing in halftime, his trips home now just brief, cushiony dreams.

It was World Progeria Day. Everything had a hashtag; you could die by hashtag. The Breath maintained its constancy, hovering around Jakub like plastic sheeting come to life. To drown it out, in his head, he listed off fatal conditions and emergencies. Heart disease. Lung cancer. Mouth cancer. Diabetes. Mental illness: schizophrenia, suicidal tendencies. Stroke. Parkinson's. Celiac. ALS. Each had its own dedicated foundation, an organization to fight it, educate the public, raise awareness. Each had its own day—its own thirst for engagement, to be spoken aloud and so rendered a bit less lethal.

A ping alerted him to the presence of two new emails in his inbox. The first was from a Monica in Human Resources.

I am trying to locate a delivery of 6 boxes of paper to the EA Bldg. today. It should have been delivered to the 5th Floor, but was delivered to another floor by mistake, can you please let me know if this was received on your floor. Thanks very much.

The second was Code White. *Unsafe situation. Aggression. A patient or visitor presents a violent threat towards self or others.*

Please remain calm. Please remain calm.

◆

One day, he went to stand beside Karyn's desk to wait for her to stop chewing on her shirt, which was protocol on EA5 when you had a question or request. After a few minutes of staring intently at her screen, Karyn turned, lowered the moistened hem of a wraparound sweater, and said, "What's up?"

There's a man in the boiler room. Sucking the life from everyone.

"The server is being funny," Jakub said. *Can't you hear it?*

"'Kay," she said. "I.T.?"

Jakub nodded and went back to his desk. *Query made; open a ticket.*

Find the man in the boiler room. Determine his intentions. Find out if he's a threat.

"In It for Life!," Kelly chirped behind him. The clacking of fingernails on keys.

◆

On the roof of the parking garage, he calculated the variables: the height of the structure, his weight, the angle of his body against the wind and against the pavement. A gust rocked him forward, closer to the brick barrier that was low enough for a six-year-old to climb. Below him, the wings of the health centre sprawled out toward a heavily treed enclave of mansions. The highway ran beside it, carrying the common people past the sick and dying in a silent, oblivious parade. Jakub realized he was grinding his teeth. His stomach and his jaw were in a clench. The wind rushed past his ears, raw blasts of uncontrollable sound. Only wind could drown out the Breath. The rushing of gravity's wind. The last sensation, wet and explosive. A sharp introduction of silence.

Kelly, watching from EA5. Mouthing to him across the void:

Code Orange... Disaster!

◆

He knew he would have to go back to the boiler room. The Breath was an answer to everything and nothing. It was up to Jakub to interpret the grotesquerie. But he needed someone to talk to about it.

On a day when crisp, miniscule granules of ice fell slowly from the grey sky, Jakub walked the windowed hall of G-wing, the wooden soles of his black dress shoes knocking on the concrete. The light made everything the colour of old bone. He expected to see Amir there at the end, sitting in his usual spot, but the hallway was empty, save for a lone nurse fussing with a tray of bottles and steel instruments. Jakub smiled at her to catch her eye, made sure his badge was visible.

"Excuse me," he said. *Acknowledge.* "My name is Jakub." *Introduce.* "Quick question for you." *Duration.* "Do you know a patient named Amir? He often sits here, in his chair." *Explanation.*

The nurse's all-business mask softened when she heard the name, becoming somber.

"Yes," she said. "Of course."

"I know this is well beyond protocol, but do you know where I might find him? I work in the EA building. For the centre. It's, ah, a communications question."

She refocused on Jakub, a sad look in her eyes.

"He—he passed," she said. "Yesterday."

Jakub stood silent.

She glanced down at his badge.

"You're in communications," she said. "Thought you'd have known."

He couldn't hide the question that showed on his face: *why would I know that the man I'm asking after is dead?*

"It was MAID," said the nurse. "Only the second case at the Centre. Big kerfuffle, attracted a lot of media."

"I was just talking to him," said Jakub. "Not... long ago. What's MAID?"

The nurse gave him a strange look and went back to fiddling with bottles. "Medical Assistance in Dying," she said. She stood back, wiped her hands on her scrubs. "With some diseases, it's hard to see how much a person is suffering. Imagine, being you, with your own brain working just fine, but your body can't hear you anymore? It just stops responding. That's what ALS does to you. It's brutal. Sorry... if you knew him, I mean."

Code Yellow: Missing Person.

Jakub nodded weakly. The ducts above roared to life and began to issue their low-frequency moan. The Breathing Man had joined the conversation, offering lament or confession, threat or plea.

◆

The Breath told him where to go. Back up the corridor of G-wing. Past the elevator bay, down the hallway leading away from the cafeteria. Occasionally, other sounds impinged: the din of nurses chatting together on their break. The wheels of a cart rumbling over linoleum. Bells and chimes sounding over the public address system, preceding the declaration of different codes. But, at base, the great bellows of Breath ploughed ever-outward and inward, driving him around corners, down passages, past the tiny nook of the Spiritual Care office and the locked double doors of the Adult Mental Health unit—the most shameful inadequacies tucked away in the deepest regions of the hospital—until he reached the inconspicuous sign that read MORGUE.

There was no one inside. The Breath welcomed him with monstrous amplitude, as though its waves had surged in and cleared everyone from the stark, windowless space. The hospital morgue was at once simpler and ghastlier than he'd imagined, a trio of nondescript beige offices bordering a hallway that led to a polished steel door, beyond which he found the row of metal embalming tables, the pulleys and braces hanging above each, the shelves crowded with tubs full of silver hooks, needles, spigots. The broad, walk-in closet at the back, where white plastic buckets were stacked like pagoda towers, housing their brined extractions. Each conveniently labeled by date, name and specimen, so that it took Jakub no time at all to find what he needed.

You wish for another body.

It should have been delivered to the 5th Floor, but was delivered to another

The best way to find yourself—

◆

10% buffered formalin. A half dozen toxicity labels. The liquid sloshed as Jakub placed the bucket down on the concrete, so he could prepare his gift before opening the door. There was formality to be observed, for both donor and host.

The bucket's lid popped off with a wet *plok!* Threatening vapors wafted up. He breathed them in, keeping time with the greater Breath, his guide and master.

What is it, thought Jakub, *that makes us nurture what consumes us?*

He lifted the pale, wet lungs from the bucket and cradled them, so that they lay like a butchered fawn across his forearms, one sallow lobe draped over each wrist. With his foot, he pushed the boiler room door, and walked forward into the murk.

The Breathing Man took no notice of Jakub, fixed as he was on the task of recycling the air of the EA building through lungs choked with scurf, anguish, abandonment, decay. The shuddering frequencies of the Breath made the room vibrate, sending tiny flakes of skin from his contorted body to join the motes drifting in the murk. Jakub knelt before the man, head bowed. Volatile liquid seeped into Jakub's khaki trousers, the scent of formalin hovering, miasmic, around the lungs they held like a sacred altar.

"I brought these," he said, loud enough to be heard over the Breath. "For you."

It was only a hiccup. A catch in the cascade of noise. Yet there was no mistake: Jakub's words had, however briefly, caught the Breathing Man's attention. Maybe they could still find a way through the fear. Maybe they could take care of each other.

When the Breath stopped suddenly, the silence rang in Jakub's ears like a wine glass struck with a stray tooth.

The Breathing Man had turned to face Jakub, the swampy cataracts of his eyes focusing on this penitent and his gift. Small, shallow rasps had replaced the Breath. His chest rose and fell like that of a dying calf; the skin of his belly was like parchment, revealing the bowels underneath. His ribs were a haunted circus tent of crooked slats and drooping skin.

With a ropy, white finger, he reached down slowly, and tapped Jakub once, twice, three times on the chest, in time with the rise and fall of Jakub's lungs, which he realized were operating at a skewed pant, nothing like his normal rhythm, as though a dial were being turned up to test their compatibility with an unfamiliar system.

Not enough, he thought, feeling the damp weight on his knees, the pickled organs that were not his gift to give. From across the divide, Amir's ghost smiled at him. *It can mean many things, to care.*

As the Breathing Man's fingers sunk into his chest, pushing through skin, suctioning through blood and digging at the fascia to get to the ribcage and the living lungs underneath, Jakub tried as he could, but could think of no code to declare.

A RED PROMISE IN THE PALM OF YOUR HAND

JOSH ROUNTREE

CLASP my hands in prayer as Mr. Amos sews wings onto my dead brother's shoulders. Mr. Amos approaches his task with care. He works the catgut thread in and out of Robert's skin, pulling every stitch taut. He is carrying out God's plan, though I'm not sure what god he means anymore. We abandoned our Christian god sometime back, just as the Christian god abandoned us.

So claims Mr. Amos, in any event.

This is wrong, Bess.

Mother's voice again. She is two years dead, but her spirit remains. This clapboard house is her living corpse. The wind presses against the walls and gives her breath. She speaks through groaning timbers and the door clattering in its broken frame.

In the evenings, wind rushes down through the stone chimney and becomes her screams.

These creatures fly in the face of creation.

Mother sounds bitter, but that doesn't necessarily mean she's wrong.

"Bess. Help me, please?" Mr. Amos waves me over, bites off the thread with an eye tooth, fastens the last knot. "Get his feet, if you would."

Mr. Amos wears dusty black pants and a once-white shirt, now a ruin of brown stains. His eyes are sunk deep into his sun-red face, but they forever skip across the surface of the world like a flat stone on a lake, never still. He chews at a matchstick, rolling it back and forth between his teeth.

Mr. Amos grabs Robert's torso, I lift his legs, and together we haul him outside. His small body is easy enough to move, even with its new appendages.

The stone waits for us, black with old blood, an upcropping of flat granite in the rough shape of a triangle, about ten feet long. Mr. Amos said this stone table was a holy place for the Comanches, but we have lived here on the edge of the Llano since Robert was a baby, and we've never seen a Comanche. Mother believed they were frightened of this place. Mr. Amos is confident the new god we've brought with us into the wilderness keeps any outsiders at bay.

I'm no longer certain if we brought our god with us or if He was here already, waiting.

We position Robert on the stone table and Mr. Amos stands back, hands on his hips.

"I envy that boy," he says. "Those are good wings."

Robert lies on his back and the wings fan out on either side, each of them three feet long. They're crafted of mesquite limbs and animal hides, rib bones and clay. I helped Mr. Amos with their creation. If my brother was to die, I intended for him to have the finest wings I could provide.

"Your mother would be proud of her beautiful boy."

My mother has told me what she thinks of this, but I'm the only one who still hears her. Or maybe the only one who listens.

"It's getting close to dark," I say.

The sun sits fat and red against the horizon. Long shadows grow from the row of houses, situated in an arc around the stone table. Loose boards rattle, and the roofs have been torn away from the houses that used to belong to the Lancasters and the Hendersons. Our empty stock pen is a mess of leaning mesquite pickets and overgrown scrub brush. The wind stalks the flat earth. Used to be we cared for this home we built for ourselves, but there have been too few of us left to do that for a long time.

I know we can't be out here after dark, but I need another moment with my brother. I comb his hair with my fingers, moving it out of his eyes. He's cold in spite of the late summer heat, and his skin is already growing gray and bloated. His body yawns red from chest to stomach, and the bloody knife that made the killing cut hangs from Mr. Amos's belt. I don't feel the kind of anguish I've been expecting, but then again, I've been mourning Robert since before his death.

"Let's go, Bess," Mr. Amos says. "Don't want to get caught out after dark."

No, we definitely do not want to get caught out.

◆

We butchered the last of our pigs earlier in the summer and now Mr. Amos and I finish off the shank with a side of snap peas and hard bread. We dine from the remnants of Mother's china, brought with us from Austin—red roses faded to pink, gold gilt chipping away from the edges. The china was handed down from her grandmother, and it was the only thing Mother insisted on bringing with us, no matter how impractical. Mr. Amos encouraged every one of us to release our worldly possessions before we set off into the wilderness. And so we had, save for that china.

"We shall both follow young Robert, whither he goes." Mr. Amos attempts to smile, but it's weighed down by his gray moustache. "You and I will find glory too."

We both know Mr. Amos is too old to follow. Where he will go when he passes is a mystery.

God only gives flight to the young.

"If I'm the next chosen to serve, my killing will be up to you," he says. "Your hands must be quick, and they must be steady. You're a faithful girl. You'll be up to the task."

There used to be so many of us living in this wilderness. Now it's just Mr. Amos and me. I've given

no thought to what will happen if I am the last of us alive. My only concern is whether our god will accept me if I'm chosen. I am nearly seventeen and there is some question as to whether I'm a child or an adult. No adult in our community has ever been granted flight. Now the possibility of outliving everyone else burns in my mind like a fever.

Kill him before he kills you. Do it tonight.

I ignore my mother's voice and clear away the dishes while Mr. Amos ensures every window is shuttered, the door firmly barred. The wind beats against the house, causing it to groan and shriek, and since the wind never relents, neither do my mother's admonishments.

Listen to me, Bess. They're monsters.

Every shuddering board gives her voice, and she grows louder as darkness falls.

We were wrong to come here. I'm sorry.

I wash the dishes while Mr. Amos sits in a low chair by the fire, rolling a cigarette. The bone jar sits on the roughhewn cedar mantle, a heavy thing made of murky green glass and filled with rib bones we all collected from the land. The bones are sun-whitened and brittle, save for one stained red with blood. It waits there for each of us, like eternity. Just as cold and just as uncertain. Robert was the last one to pull the red bone from the jar, and soon enough Mr. Amos and I will gather around it and take our turns again.

Mr. Amos smokes his cigarette and retires early to his bed, as is his habit. I situate myself in his vacated chair by the fire and listen for them to arrive.

It would be no sin to drive the carving knife into his chest while he sleeps.

Once, Mother was the most devout of us all, but she lost her faith. I'm not sure what to believe anymore. Only Mr. Amos remains to guide me in matters of the spirt, and his gospel now carries the taint of desperation.

I hear the sound of heavy wings in flight, then something thumps against the roof. This pattern is repeated until I count at least seven of the fliers on our roof, and many more in the yard. In my mind they circle Robert, eager to receive him. They are angels with golden halos and mournful eyes. Their soft hands lift my brother's body and urge him to flight.

Mr. Amos snores from his sleeping loft, his rest aided by a dram of whisky.

I'm wide awake.

Mother has gone quiet, thinking perhaps they won't remember her. This ploy is never effective.

Right away, the fliers on our roof begin to pick at the shingles, hammering with hands and feet and wings. Others batter the walls, loosening the clapboard siding. All of this elicits a scream from my mother that makes me question everything I've been taught.

Why did she abandon her beliefs? Why did she abandon Robert and me? Her miserable afterlife is her own fault, and yet that doesn't keep me from mourning her sad state.

This commotion carries on for several minutes, and then the fliers are gone as quickly as they came. Mother's screams continue for most of the night.

She is my mother, so I listen, and try not to judge.

◆

We spend the next morning pretending at normal life.

There are no animals left to be tended, but there are weeds to be pulled from the garden and water to be hauled from the nearby creek. Mr. Amos climbs onto the roof with a hammer and nails, working to undo the damage from the night before. His efforts are pointless. He labors against the inevitable. The house can never be what it was, and what is repaired will only be pulled apart again. The fliers will rend Mother's spirit just as they did her body. But to Mr. Amos, the house is nothing more than shelter, and the work keeps him busy. He's a man quickly running out of purpose, and it would be cruel to take anything else away from him.

Robert's body is gone from the stone table. I place my hands where we'd laid him, and the rock is hot to the touch. I consider what it will feel like to be left there. To open my eyes to the afterlife with all of my friends eager to accept me.

I move about my tasks in a malaise, muddled by lack of sleep and wishing for the time when there were others to share the labor.

Thirteen families founded this community. Seventy-four people in all, including my mother, my brother, and me. My father passed not long after Robert was born, and his death broke Mother. It was Mr. Amos who seemingly put her together again, with his sermons about the failure of our old religion and the promise of the new. And when they took up together in a family away, his whole congregation celebrated. It was Mother's decision as much as his for all of us to leave Austin and build a life someplace beyond the reach of human judgement. When I was little more than a toddler, we all rode out together, and kept going until Mr. Amos found the stone table and assured us that we had reached our Eden.

Paradise proved to be hot and dusty and difficult, but this place was ours, and we were all glad to have it. No matter the cost.

Everything according to His plan.

Late in the morning I call Mr. Amos off the roof for a glass of water. We stand together in the shade of the covered porch, both of us withered by the summer heat. Age has whittled him down to bones and his long hair has gone gray.

We share in the silence. I miss the slow, struggling whine of the windmill, its mechanism now seized up and several of its blades rusting in the tall yellow weeds. A plow languishes in the field. I miss the good-natured chatter of families working toward a shared goal. Quails used to scamper through the brush, and mockingbirds called from the trees, but even they have left this place. And while the mesquites and sticker burrs and other hard things still cling to the cracked earth, everything worth loving here has long since blown away.

Everything is dying, as if the land itself ushers us toward our inevitable conclusion.

"God be good. They accepted him into the fold." Mr. Amos motions with his glass to the empty stone table.

"Robert was always a faithful child." I recite the words he expects from me, though I'm not sure Robert was old enough to understand that kind of faith.

"That he was. And smart as a whip, too." Mr. Amos makes a sharp face as he bites back the alkaline taste of the water. "That boy could light up your mother's eyes. She loved him so." Talk of Mother clouds his expression with sadness, and he shakes his head, like he's trying to dislodge bad memories.

"Yes, she was fond of him," I say. "She loved us all, but I think Robert was her special one."

Mr. Amos smiles. "Might be he was."

"Mr. Amos, I feel some uncertainty."

"We're every one of us uncertain. That's why faith is so necessary."

"I think what I mean to say is, I'm not prepared for this. Maybe I'll be chosen first, but the Lord could call for you next and then I'll be by myself."

"That is a possibility."

"Who'll sew my wings when it's my time?"

"The Lord will provide," he says.

"Is there any other course of action we might take? Some way both of us could live. With His blessing, of course. Must we carry this through to the end?"

Mr. Amos has been watching a bit of dust spin up and dance along the horizon, but my words sharpen his attention, and he puts a leathery hand on my shoulder like he's afraid I might bolt.

"There is no other path to walk. Don't go looking for one."

My mother went looking for one. The fliers found her, brought her body back in pieces, and left it in the yard.

"I wouldn't," I say. "I won't."

"We'll carry on as we always have. And this will end as we've always known it would."

The big knife never leaves Mr. Amos's hip; it lives there as a promise about exactly how this will end.

"Yes sir, I suppose it will."

Mr. Amos hands me his glass and climbs back onto the roof. The sound of his hammer echoes through the afternoon. When he comes back down for dinner, he reveals the Lord's command.

We're drawing bones tonight.

◆

In the evening we place the bone jar between us on the dining table and plunge our hands inside, removing the bones, one by one. We close our eyes as we draw. We open them to reveal if one of us has chosen the red bone, or if we must draw again.

The drawing of bones used to be a festive event in our community, one accompanied by laughter and good food. Chicken and potatoes with butter. Fried okra and pies with freshly harvested pecans. All of us gathered around in anticipation as Mr. Keller played his guitar and sang godly songs. Whether we drew our bones in the dusty sunlight with cicadas in chorus around us or beneath gray clouds, earth dusted with snow, the bone jar held a ceremonial position on the stone table. All of us surrounding it, taking our turns, until the selection of one soul was met with joy, and a measure of hidden sadness. A tightness always came to my

chest. I'd close my eyes and breathe slowly, catching the smell of juniper and wildflowers on the breeze, and I was never certain whether to feel disappointed or quietly happy that I hadn't been chosen.

I still can't say which was right.

Over time, our numbers dwindled, and I began to wonder whether His most devout servants were taken first, or if He left the best of us for last.

Maybe our god wouldn't take everyone.

Then the fliers hunted down my mother, and I knew that none of us were leaving here by any method other than His.

Mr. Amos and I have no energy left for fanfare. Tonight, we eat cold dried beef and hard biscuits. We draw the bones not beneath the summer sky, but by the uncertain light of a guttering candle.

Mr. Amos appears upset about our earlier conversation. It's not the first time I've prodded at the edges of our faith, but never so overtly. He approaches our ceremony in workmanlike fashion, opening his eyes to reveal each bloodless bone in his hand, then tossing it to the floor with a grunt. He's going at the whisky harder than is his nature, and it clouds his eyes. If he has a preference whether he lives or dies, it's impossible to tell.

When the jar is half empty and the oak floorboards are littered with rib bones, one of us is finally chosen.

I open my eyes, and there it is. A red promise in the palm of my hand.

Mr. Amos stares at the bone, his mouth slightly open. His breathing is raspy, like something coarse is trying to escape his throat. He washes it back with whisky from the bottle and finds his words.

"It'll be you then."

Run away, Bess!

Mr. Amos turns his head, listens. Like he's hearing her for the first time. Decides it's only the wind.

You'll be damned if you let him gut you. You'll be one of them.

I am damned already, whether she sees that or not. That choice was made the moment we rode out from Austin.

"Do you need help with your wings?" Mr. Amos asks.

I shake my head, still holding the red bone.

I can build them myself.

◆

I spend most of the next day building my wings.

They are not so grand as the ones I made for Robert. Stiff leather lashed to a frame of rusted baling wire. A few chicken feathers and some mesquite bark. They will function, perhaps, but they're not beautiful.

Mr. Amos busies himself with any task he can find. He's stopped speaking to me, and I'm not certain what's happening in his mind. My own thoughts center on his knife parting my breastbone, and his methodical hands working at my back with hammer and awl, like a saddle maker. When he places my body on the stone table, will the fliers come for me like they have all of the other children, or will I be harshly judged?

Will they recognize me as a child at all?

This question consumes me as the afternoon shadows grow long and Mr. Amos takes a seat on the front porch, sharpening his long knife against a whetstone.

Every one of us is given wings and offered to Him on the stone table, but only children are blessed with flight. When the night grows dark and the living have barricaded themselves inside our homes, the fliers bleed new life into the children and lift them up among their number. The adults, in their hubris, all believe they are faithful enough to join these angels. But every one of them is torn asunder. Their new wings are shredded. Little remains of them but blood and a few bones.

I haul my wings inside our home. Mr. Amos offers me a nod when I pass. The steady rasp of his knife against the stone counts down the seconds of my life.

Mother's voice is sullen. *Stupid girl.*

I place my wings carefully in the corner and take a seat in one of the dining chairs. "*My* choices aren't what brought us here."

You could have left.

The lie is so bold that I don't bother responding.

I tried my best. I love you.

"You tried to leave, and you didn't take us with you. You didn't even tell us you were going."

Your stepfather's faith is fierce. I was too afraid.

"Are you afraid now?" I asked. "When the fliers come?"

Yes.

"When I'm a flier, I'll pick at your bones too."

"Who are you talking to?" Mr. Amos stands in the doorway.

"My mother."

His face wrinkles up, unsure what to make of this. A few seconds later, he thinks he has it sorted, and he nods his head. "It's good to pray."

"I'm a faithful girl."

"Bess, we'll need to get on with this now, if I'm to finish the work before nightfall."

He might as well be talking about whitewashing the siding or digging a few postholes for all the emotion he reveals. I remember the quiet way he reassured Robert at the end, the way he calmed him by humming one of the old hymns. Robert was resolute, right up until the moment Mr. Amos drew his knife, and then I had to hold my brother tight to keep him from running. That knife tore a wet scream loose from Robert's lungs.

The sound still haunts me.

Mr. Amos walks closer, and there's no one to hold me in place. I stand and scamper away. Terror gnaws at the structure of my faith.

"I don't think I'm ready, Mr. Amos."

"Our day is chosen for us," he says. "The decision is not ours."

Kill him!

"I don't want to," I say.

Mr. Amos unsheathes his knife.

"It'll be okay, Bess. I swear by the love I have for you children and for your mother that I'll do this quick. You won't suffer none."

Wind crashes from the west and Mother rages. Her words become incoherent. Her will is immaterial. The heat of death suffuses her corpse, and I want nothing more right now than to escape from inside her. If I could wish myself into never having been born, I'd make that choice in an instant, but there is not enough love or faith remaining in the world to compel me toward my own death.

In the end, my fear wins out.

I back myself up against the stone fireplace as Mr. Amos advances. He whispers words of comfort that I cannot hear over Mother's anger. The bone jar waits there on the mantle. Useless now. There will never be another drawing. Mr. Amos will most likely die a lonely old man, forever wondering why he was the last of us.

He slides the rocking chair out of the way, close enough now that I can smell last night's whisky.

His lips grasp at prayers.

Mr. Amos clenches his jaw and the wiry muscles in his neck grow taut beneath the stubble of his beard. He tries to get a hand on me, to hold me still, but he doesn't expect a real fight.

I reach for the bone jar, heft it over my head. The green glass is thick and heavy. When I bring it down against his face with everything I have, Mr. Amos drops like he's been shot.

The jar slips from my hands, shatters against the floor. Bones scatter like insects from beneath an overturned rock. Green glass shards swim in the blood that flows like water from the broken dam of Mr. Amos's skull. The right side of his head is a red ruin, and his wide-open eyes are hazy with death. I had no intention of killing him, but I've done it anyway. The walls rattle around me, and Mother's voice stirs up the smell of stale woodsmoke.

I love you. Bess. Please leave. Before they get here.

I can't leave. That much I know.

So, instead, I do what I was raised to do.

◆

I'm sweaty and exhausted by the time I've attached my wings to Mr. Amos's back and dragged his body to the stone table. I whisper prayers over his still form. The old man was faithful to the last, and I hope our god finds him worthy in ways the others were not.

I tell him I'm sorry, but *sorry* solves nothing.

Night crowds in from all sides. Wind whistles through the carcass of what used to be our community. A year or two after we're all gone, the wilderness will have reclaimed every inch. All the meat, all the life, chewed away. None of us will even be a memory. I wonder what our life here has been for, and I suppose that is where our faith must provide the answers, but when our spirits have fled and even the fliers have abandoned this place, who'll be left to care? I sit on the stone table beside Mr. Amos, losing myself in this melancholy, until I hear a sound like storm winds tossing a mainsail, and I know the fliers are close.

I slide down off the stone table and run to our house.

Inside, Mother shrieks, but I no longer listen to what she says. She has failed me, but in these last desperate moments I have decided not to fail her. I won't endure another night of her soul being twisted and torn. If I'm to leave this place, which I mean to do one way or another, I won't abandon her. I won't let her insides fill up with rats and horned toads and muddy wasp nests. She won't face eternity here alone.

I rummage through the pantry until I find the cannister of kerosene on the bottom shelf. In half a minute, the table, the chairs, the blue lace curtains, the old rocker, are all doused with the stuff. I don't know where my mother's soul will end up when this house is gone, but it can't be a worse hell than the one she's burning in now.

I strike a kitchen match. I light the whole box.

When I leave the house and slam the door behind me, Mother is already engulfed.

Wings thunder overhead, and I don't bother to hide. I spent so much time wondering if the fliers would have me, that I never considered what might happen if I was chosen and refused to die. Now my fate is no more certain than my mother's. No more certain than that of poor Mr. Amos.

If they mean to punish me, I surely deserve it.

The ground shakes as they land all around me, my angels. They crawl about on hands and feet, sniffing at the earth. Faces of bone, bodies gone gray, red tongues tasting the air. Their wings stir the smoke that billows from the burning house. A few of them whisper back and forth in a language I can't decipher. They have no interest in Mr. Amos. Instead they grab me with bent fingers and pull me to my knees. There are so many. I should be afraid, but I'm not.

I know these children. They're all my friends.

Robert crouches before me. His eyes are black holes, but his little boy smile is the same as its always been. He offers me his hand, and I take it without reservation. Pain cuts a trail up my spine and settles in my shoulder blades. The bones in my back bend and snap and shudder. They press against my insides, looking for a way to escape.

When my wings come, my screams are joyful.

The rest of them close in. So cold. So beautiful. And we rise together, into the heavens.

STILL ON OUR BULLSHIT

To Offer Her Pleasure – Ali Seay

After the death of his father and being abandoned by his mother, Ben finds a book that calls for a shadowy, horned figure. She comes with unexpected gifts and the comfort of a dependable presence. And she asks for very little in return. Sometimes, family requires more than a little sacrifice.

Things Have Gotten Worse Since We Last Spoke – Eric LaRocca

Sadomasochism. Obsession. Death.

A whirlpool of darkness churns at the heart of a macabre ballet between two lonely young women in an internet chat room in the early 2000s — a darkness that threatens to forever transform them once they finally succumb to their most horrific desires.

She Who Rules the Dead – Maria Abrams

Henry has received a message: he needs to sacrifice five people to the demon that's been talking to him in his nightmares. He already has four, and number five, Claire, is currently bound in the back of his van. Too bad Claire isn't exactly human.

Beautiful/Grotesque - edited by Sam Richard

From full-on hardcore horror to decadently surreal nightmares, and noir-fueled psychosis, to an eerie meditation on grief, and familial quiet horror, Beautiful/Grotesque guides us through the murky waters where the monstrous and the breathtaking meet. Featuring stories by Roland Blackburn, Jo Quenell, Katy Michelle Quinn, Joanna Koch, and Sam Richard.

Publishing weird horror and the grotesque since 2015.

weirdpunkbooks.com

THE MACABRE READER

BOOK REVIEWS BY
LYSETTE STEVENSON

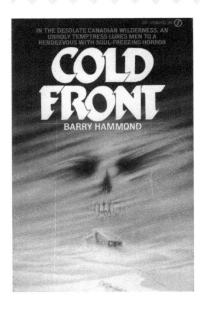

COLD FRONT
by Barry Hammond.
Cover art by Tom Hallman.
Signet Canada, 1982.

Set in the far northwestern region of Alberta, Canada; a climate infamous for its long inhospitable winters. Three oil rig workers flee from the crime of a brutal murder and robbery. With a body in the trunk, a box full of cash and enough whiskey to keep them habitually inebriated they soon find themselves lost in a blizzard with something inexplicable trailing their scent. The three men come upon the smoking chimney of a remote one room cabin and seek shelter in it from the storm. They soon discover the sole occupant is a beautiful but disconcerting woman hiding in the root cellar.

Hammond's storytelling is effectively minimalist and taut. From the start these men are antagonists; crude, brash, prone to violence and lecherous desires. You move from each character's point of view reliving the turning points in their lives that have led them to this moment of desperation and madness. What Hammond offers in abundance is a sensory overload of filth; all manner of internal fluids and gore. The novel is unrestrained in loathsome details. Terror and tension mount between the power and immensity of Nature and these characters isolated in their most base state of being. A potent work of cosmic horror.

Barry Hammond a resident of Edmonton, Alberta has served for many years as On Spec magazine's poetry editor. He has published dozens of short stories and poetry in various speculative literature anthologies. *Cold Front* is his only novel.

SOME UNKNOWN GULF OF NIGHT
by W. H. Pugmire
with wrap-around cover art by contemporary symbolist painter Matthew Jaffe published by Arcane Wisdom, 2011.

Written as an impassioned response to Lovecraft's early 1930's sonnet sequence, *The Fungi of Yuggoth*. Here W. H. Pugmire takes on the role of the psychopomp ushering the reader into his vision of the

Lovecraftian dream world. Once acquiring a grimoire of hidden lore, you arrive at the witching hour on the borderland of an eldritch wood. The path beckons further to an ancient graveyard where Nyarlathotep waits. Pugmire infuses the prose-poems with a queerness and eroticism not explicitly found in H. P. Lovecraft's work. Along with generous homages to Chambers' *The King in Yellow*, Wilum achieves something wholly new. It is beneficial to read both poets' cycles in tandem to each other but slowly and with deliberation. Give each piece time to steep before carrying on as these 36 vignettes are so decadently worked they are truly bewitching. My personal experience is they are best read aloud to feel the full richness of language and grotesque beauty.

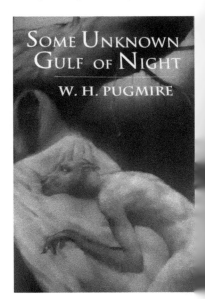

March 26, 2019 the world became less wild and luminous as the ever talented and iconic Wilum Hopfrog Pugmire passed on into the Dreamlands. Wilum's extraordinary gift as a poet not only reflected in his craft but as one of those few remarkable souls that lived their life as Art. A true individual whose inspired work will live on for generations to come.

GOSSAMER DAYS: SPIDERS, HUMANS AND THEIR THREADS
by Eleanor Morgan
published by Strange Attractor Press, 2016.

While I was reading Dr. Leo Martello's classic 1960's text: *Weird Ways of Witchcraft*, I came across an obscured black and white photograph of a man who belonged to a secret society in Vanuatu. At first glance he appeared to be shrouded in a thick bedding of dreadlocks until I read the caption that it was in fact a headdress made of spider webs. I immediately went on a hunt to verify if this was real and found Eleanor Morgan's book, *Gossamer Days*.

As an artist, Eleanor collected spider silk to use in her creative endeavors. Through her own anthropological research she uncovered a rich history of humans working with the remarkable properties of gossamer. Either used as the fine lines of telescope and rifle sites, or ethereal Victorian portraits made from cobweb canvases. To an illustrious golden cape that took eight years to weave in Madagascar and is kept in archive at the Royal Albert Museum in London. My initial curiosity was sated when I reached the chapters on the remote islands of the Pacific. Here the indigenous tribes use the abundance of golden orb silk to make ceremonial masks and shaman robes. As well as smothering hoods; where widows are ritually suffocated at their husbands funeral to join them in the afterlife and criminal offenses are handled by filling the cobweb hood with live spiders to cap the offenders face.

While both alluring and horrifying, *Gossamer Days* is beautifully narrated, impressive in history and draws surprisingly intimate parallels between human ingenuity and the industrious arachnid many fear to love.

THE DOLL MAKER
by Sarban,
first published 1953.

Set in a girls boarding school over a seemingly endless and gloomy winter, a young woman's stay is extended as she is tutored for admission to Oxford. Lonely without her peers, feeling orphaned by her parents and oppressed by the watchful eye of the headmistress. She gains a sense of autonomy by sneaking out at night and climbing over the stone wall that separates the school grounds from the dense and wild woodland. There one evening she encounters a young man walking in the forest surrounded by what she believes to be a magical conjuring of fae lights. The student begins taking Latin lessons with the young man's mother and spending more time off the school grounds in their arcane domicile deep within the forest. What ensues is a creepy vampiric tale of submission and domination between this promising young woman and the charismatic Doll Maker.

Sarban, pseudonym John William Wall, was a British diplomat in the Middle East who largely avoided the public eye as an enigmatic writer of strange tales. He only released a scant handful of short stories and novellas originally released

in nondescript hardcover and pulp paperback, later reproduced in stunning editions by Tartarus Press, UK.

POSSESSED: THE SECRET OF MYSLOTCH

by Witold Gombrowicz in English translated from French by J. A. Underwood originally published in Polish, 1939.

Possessed was written as a satirical take on gothic horror yet it succeeds in being a macabre thrill ride. A young man travels by train to a manor estate to coach the young lady of the house on her tennis game. They feel an uncanny albeit volatile attraction to one another while her jealous fiance observes their courtship. The countryside manor perches near a formidable castle inhabited by a mad Prince. Rumors circulate of a possible treasure trove of art history wealth hidden within the castle and a locked room that contains a haunted tea towel. The young man, a professor and a clairvoyant all attempt to unravel the mystery of the sealed room and what past transgressions plague the tormented prince. *Possessed* oozes with atmosphere. Menacing and at times hilarious with truly unsettling flashes of the protagonists succumbing to a ghastly influence. At turns pulpy, literary and absurd it is an offbeat entry in the gothic genre.

Witold Gombrowicz is better known for his surrealist nightmare masterpiece, Ferdydurke. He had originally published *Possessed* as a serial under the pseudonym Zdzisław Niewieski. In the month leading up to Hitler's invasion of Poland, Gombrowicz fled to Argentina before the third installment ever made it to press. Possibly due to embarrassment that he wrote something for mass appeal, he didn't claim authorship of it until shortly before his death in 1969. It wouldn't be until 1990 that it was compiled into a complete novel format and later successfully adapted for the stage.

HOUSE OF PSYCHOTIC WOMEN: AN AUTOBIOGRAPHICAL TOPOGRAPHY OF FEMALE NEUROSIS IN HORROR AND EXPLOITATION FILMS

by Kier-La Janisse published by FAB Press, 2012.

House of Psychotic Women is a chimera in book form. A brazenly honest autobiography, exploitation horror history, cinema critique and coffee table art book. Kier-La reflects on her wayward youth growing up in Winnipeg, Manitoba; in and out of foster homes and reformatory schools. This coming of age experience drew her to the fringe portrayals of women in horror cinema, where in them she found a sense of validation, empowerment and catharsis. With her encyclopedic knowledge of underground film, a clear and deadpan delivery juxtaposed against beautifully reproduced cinema stills; the House resonates as a deeply personal narrative while illuminating an often misunderstood aspect of female experience and psychology. As well it tantalizes with a trove of cult films to seek out. Bringing all of these elements together you are immersed in a fascinating tome that is still to this day a seminal work, singular in its vision and its execution.

As a writer, director and film programmer Kier-La Janisse may be one of the most influential pioneers in the critical analysis of cult cinema. Founder of The Miskatonic Institute of Horror Studies and Montreal based Spectacular Optical Press, she has co-authored numerous books and directed/produced the 2021 folk horror documentary, *Woodland Dark and Days Bewitched*, winning the Midnighters Audience Award at SXSW.

2022 will see an expanded twentieth anniversary edition of the *House of Psychotic Women*, re-released through British publisher FAB Press.

TALES OF THE GROTESQUE: A COLLECTION OF UNEASY TALES
by L. A. Lewis,
first published 1934.

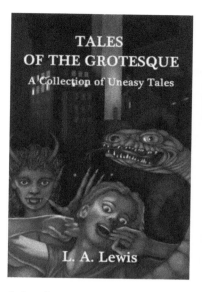

As art imitates life, Lewis himself was beset by hallucinations, suicide attempts and subsequent institutionalization. He unfortunately burned many of his later manuscripts. What remained is a mixture of distinctive horror written in a period between the wars that are startlingly gruesome even by today's standards.

Published in both ghost story collections and Theosophical periodicals, his supernatural tales show this latter influence unabashedly. With occult detectives, spiritualist seances, powers of clairvoyance; overtly layered in the characters' conversations regarding the veiled nature of reality. Lewis was a fighter pilot in both world wars for the British Royal Air Force. Several stories feature pilot encounters with strange phenomena such as the air fighter Gremlin folklore to cursed planes that carry their own malevolent sentience. Other stories center on serial killers, river portals, hybrid man/bird beasts, sadistic wraiths, lunatic asylum escapees and religious cults. His multifarious imagination rose above the typical ghost tales in the early half of the twentieth century.

For decades little was known biographically about L. A. Lewis until the late editor Richard Dalby connected with his widow. Mrs. Lewis not only filled in the historical gaps but bequeathed the literary copyrights to Mr. Dalby. In her honor, he was able to bring this collection multiple times back into print.

A LONG, DARK, GRIM ROAD
by Joseph S. Pulver, Sr.
Cover art etchings by Dave Felton. Published by the Lovecraft eZine Press, 2018.

At only 28 pages in length what this work has in brevity of print it makes up for in spades by its grueling rhythm and visceral experience. You are taken on a ruthless journey through the witch haunted vales of Russia where dark forces and the darker men of God tread. Three men are traveling by horse and coach en route to Moscow. The forest looms over them and the roads are treacherous. Nightly they seek shelter amidst the fearful and destitute country folk. The deep night is filled with menace as they feign sleep to the cries of growlings, other wolves and grey leeches. Heathens are granted salvation via the barrel end of an American Winchester rifle, well honed blades or purification by fire. Fueled by a feverous sense of virtue and revenge these monstrous men persist. This sinister world of ancient corruption adds to the ever ravening greater Mythos.

Joe Pulver was a titan in the field of weird horror and neo-noir. A writer, poet, editor and champion of promoting new voices, sadly this was the last work he saw put to print before he passed away in Berlin, April 24th 2020. Joe leaves this world with a visionary legacy of work that will stand the test of time and is a gift to those who have yet to discover it.

ABBERANT VISIONS

FILM REVIEWS BY
TOM GOLDSTEIN

4X4 (2019)
Starring: Peter Lanzani, Dady Brieva, Luis Brandoni
Director: Mariano Cohn
Writers: Mariano Cohn, Gaston Duprat
Running time: 88 minutes

A man breaks into an SUV to steal anything he can. But he can't get out, no matter what he smashes. The vehicle has been sound-proofed and fitted with windows that allow occupants to see, but not be seen.

Eventually the car's owner contacts the thief and informs him that his fate is squarely in the hands of the owner. A darkly comic and ironic Argentine tale of creative vigilante justice.

PIETA (2012)
Starring: Min-soo Jo, Lee Jung-jin, Ki-Hong Woo, et. al.
Director: Ki-duk Kim
Writer: Ki-duk Kim
Running time: 103 minutes

Back in the day, South Korean film-makers wrote the book on revenge-based morality plays. Pieta is a prime example, if somewhat more extreme.

A brutal, cold-blooded enforcer for a loanshark has his life thrown into disarray when a woman shows up, claiming to be the mother who abandoned him as an infant 30 years earlier. There's a bit of David Mamet in the screenplay, although it veers into areas the American playwright likely wouldn't consider.

The movie is an examination of what a person is willing to lose for love, money or revenge. The result is un-flinchingly brutal, with a dollop of twisted black humour.

THE CLOSET (2020)
Starring: Jung-woo Ha, Yool Heo, Nam-gil Kim
Director: Kwang-bin Kim
Writer: Kwang-bin Kim
Running time: 97 minutes

A recently-widowed architect and his tween daughter move into a new home. Their fragile relationship takes a dark turn when the girl disappears into her closet (literally). Reminiscent of Asian horror films like Ringu and Ju-on, The Closet examines the emotional carnage parents sometimes inflict on their children, often with good intentions and without realizing the effect. This Korean film is more cerebral than visceral and should satisfy those who appreciate that kind of approach.

THE PLACE OF NO WORDS (2019)
Starring: Mark Webber, Teresa Palmer, Bodhi Palmer
Director: Mark Webber
Writer: Mark Webber
Running time: 95 minutes

What happens when we die? This fantasy/drama deals with the question through the eyes of a three-year-old boy whose father is terminally ill. The movie shifts between scenes of a rugged Viking fantasy world filled with fairies, ogres and "farting" ponds and the real world of past good times and present hospital beds. The on-screen family, btw, is a real-life one. A gentle and thought-provoking affair.

The Place of No Words

BUOYANCY (2019)
Starring: Sarm Heng, Chan Visal, Chheung Vakhim, et. al.
Director: Rodd Rathjen
Writer: Rodd Rathjen
Running time: 93 minutes

A 14-year-old Cambodian boy, tired of being ordered by his father to work long days sewing and harvesting rice, runs away in the hope of finding a better life in Thailand. He gets a hard lesson in social Darwinism when he's sold to work as a slave on a Thai fishing boat. This award-winning movie, with Khmer and Thai dialogue, works as a socio-political commentary — it may make you reconsider ordering that shrimp cocktail appetizer — and as a blueprint on how to create a killer.

WOLF OF SNOW HOLLOW (2020)
Starring: Jim Cummings, Riki Lindhome, Robert Forster, et. al.
Director: Jim Cummings
Writer: Jim Cummings
Running Time: 83 minutes

A snowy, mountain town is ravaged by a serial killer. Some think it's a werewolf; others think it's not.

What starts out as a horror story quickly turns into a study of a sheriff overwhelmed by the simple horrors of his daily life: he's an alcoholic with not-uncommon family issues and department colleagues who'd rather have the case turned over to another department. Some viewers may appreciate the dead-pan humour, others may find the characters — especially the lead — simply annoying. And anyone looking for a more straight-ahead horror movie better look elsewhere.

The Wolf of Snow Hollow

ancy

WE ARE LITTLE ZOMBIES (2019)
Starring: Keita Ninomyia, Mondo Okumura, Satoshi Mizuno, Sena Nakajima
Director: Makoto Nagahisa
Writer: Makoto Nagahisa
Running time: 120 minutes

A quartet of young Japanese teens meet at the funerals/cremations of their respective parents, none of whom died of natural causes. The new orphans commiserate, bond and form a rock band, which becomes an overnight sensation thanks, in part, to the hype/social media chatter about their personal tragedies — a couple of their tunes, sung in English, are actually pretty catchy even if the lyrics are a bit morbid. There are no "walking dead" in the movie, just the talking living. What they say is absurd, nihilistic and wise in a cynically naive way. The message may be that there is no rulebook or appropriate way to grieve. You just have to deal with it.

SHE DIES TOMORROW (2020)
Starring: Kate Lyn Sheil, Jane Adams, Chris Messina, Katie Aselton, et.al.
Director: Amy Seimetz
Writer: Amy Seimetz
Running time: 84 minutes

A young woman is certain today is her last day on earth. Starting with her friend, that conviction is passed on, infecting various people in their lives — a "virus" going viral if you will.

That her friend spends much of her time wearing pyjamas, looking at a specimen through a microscope and going to a birthday party and the emergency room, may be a central symbol.

Profound? Pretentious? That's up to the viewer to decide.

ARCHENEMY (2020)
Starring: Joe Manganiello, Skylan Brooks, Zolee Griggs, Glenn Howerton, Amy Seimetz
Director: Adam Egypt Mortimer
Writer: Adam Egypt Mortimer
Running time: 90 minutes

Max Fist is a homeless barfly who scores drinks by regaling other patrons with tales of how he is really a hero from another dimension who fell to Earth through a hole in the universe. He gets to show his true self when he comes to the aid of a young friend in this comic book sci-fi noir story about stories, story tellers and story telling which combines comic book animation and live action. The plot is nothing special, but the performances and style make the movie worth a watch.

She Dies Tomorrow

PSYCHO GOREMAN
(2020)
Starring: Nita-Josee Hanna, Owen Myre, et. al.
Director: Steven Kostanski
Writer: Steven Kostanski
Running time: 95 minutes

Psycho Goreman

Nothing less than the fate of the universe is at stake in this Canadian bizarro riff on Guardians of the Galaxy. The movie plays out like something from the overheated imagination of a young teenager who's spent too much time in front of a video screen. And that's meant in the best possible way. Visually it looks like it deserves an R-rating. But in its heart, Psycho Goreman is a PG.

CONTRIBUTORS

REX BURROWS is a writer and microbiologist. He's lived in lots of different places, most recently Washington DC.

SASWATI CHATTERJEE currently lives in New Delhi, India. A lifelong fan of the weird, the strange and the messed up, she can be found either playing video games or yelling bad opinions on Twitter at @RunaChat93. Her work has previously appeared in Daily Science Fiction and Flash Fiction Online.

S.E. CLARK is a mixed media artist and a writer living in New England. Her work has appeared in publications such as *Lady Churchill's Rosebud Wristlet, The Drum Literary Magazine, Nixes Mate Review* and more. When not writing, she can be found tending to her herb garden and baking gingerbread houses in the woods. Visit her at https://seclarkwriter.wixsite.com/aprilarium if you'd like to see more of her work.

DONYAE COLES is a horror and weird fiction author. She's had work published in Pseudopod, Nightmare Magazine, Fantasy Magazine, and others. Her forthcoming debut Gothic horror novel is slated to be released in summer of 2022. Follow her on Twitter @okokno or her website, www.donyaecoles.com.

THERESA DELUCCI's fiction has appeared or is forthcoming in *Strange Horizons, Lightspeed*, and on *Tor.com*, where she also reviews horror fiction, film, and television. She's talked pop culture on podcasts for *Wired.com* and *Den of Geek*. She talks oysters, cults, and more on Twitter @tdelucci

TOM GOLDSTEIN spent about 35 years working in various capacities in newsrooms of major newspapers across Canada—as a reporter, editor, and a couple of extracurricular stints as a music or video reviewer. He has never—and still does not—consider himself a critic. Rather he's just a guy who really likes movies, with a particular interest in "different."

ORRIN GREY is a skeleton who likes monsters as well as the author of several spooky books. His stories of ghosts, monsters, and sometimes the ghosts of monsters can be found in dozens of anthologies, including Ellen Datlow's *Best Horror of the Year*. He resides in the suburbs of Kansas City and watches lots of scary movies. You can visit him online at orringrey.com.

FERNANDO JFL is a freelance illustrator focused on horror themes inspired by the aesthetics of the 70s and 80s. He works with bands from the Brazilian underground scene, incorporating his horror vibes.

JACK LOTHIAN is a screenwriter for film and television and worked as showrunner on the HBO Cinemax series *Strike Back*. His short fiction has appeared in a number of publications, including Ellen Datlow's *The Best Horror of the Year Volume Twelve* and *Volume Thirteen, The New Flesh: A Literary Tribute to David Cronenberg* and the *Necronomicon Memorial Book*. His graphic novel *Tomorrow*, illustrated by Garry Mac, was nominated for a 2018 British Fantasy Award.

J.R. MCCONVEY's debut short story collection, *Different Beasts* (Goose Lane, 2019), won the Kobo Emerging Writer Prize for speculative fiction. His stories have been shortlisted for the Journey Prize, the Bristol Short Story Prize and the Thomas Morton Prize, and published widely in journals and magazines. He sometimes works as a journalist and media producer, and exists on social media @ jrmcconvey and on the web at jrmcconvey.com.

DAN REMPEL is an illustrator from Lawrence, KS who likes to create images that evoke mood and a sense of narrative. He is especially drawn to depicting scenes of imagination, mystery, adventure, and the macabre. Visit danrempelillustration.com to see more of his work.

JOSH ROUNTREE writes horror, fantasy, science fiction, and a lot of weird nonsense. His short fiction has appeared in numerous magazines and anthologies, including *Beneath Ceaseless Skies, PseudoPod, Realms of Fantasy*, and *A Punk Rock Future*. A new collection of his short fiction, *Fantastic Americana: Stories*, is available from Fairwood Press. Josh lives in Texas and tweets about records, books, and guitars @josh_rountree.

LYSETTE STEVENSON is a stage manager with a rural outdoor equestrian theatre company and a second-generation bookseller. She lives in British Columbia.

SIMON STRANTZAS is the author of five collections of short fiction, including *Nothing is Everything* (Undertow Publications, 2018), and editor of a number of anthologies, including *Year's Best Weird Fiction, Vol. 3*. He is the co-founder and associate editor of the irregular journal, *Thinking Horror*, and, combined, has been a finalist for four Shirley Jackson Awards, two British Fantasy Awards, and the World Fantasy Award. His fiction has appeared in numerous annual best-of anthologies, and in venues such as *Nightmare, The Dark,* and *Cemetery Dance*. In 2014, his edited anthology, *Aickman's Heirs*, won the Shirley Jackson Award. He lives with his wife in Toronto, Canada.

GORDON B. WHITE is the author of the horror/weird fiction collection *As Summer's Mask Slips and Other Disruptions,* as well as the novellas *Rookfield* and *In Her Smile, the Universe* (with Rebecca J. Allred, Feb. 2022). A graduate of the Clarion West Writers Workshop, Gordon's stories have appeared in dozens of venues, including *The Best Horror of the Year, Vol. 12* and the Bram Stoker Award® winning anthology *Borderlands 6*. He regularly contributes reviews and interviews to outlets including *Nightmare, Lightspeed,* and *The Outer Dark* podcast. You can find him online at www.gordonbwhite.com.

THE OUTER DARK
PODCAST & SYMPOSIUM

Our mission is to foster conversation and connect communities among the diverse slate of creators and audience members under the umbrella of speculative fiction - inclusive, safe and welcoming to women, LBGTQIA+, and writers of color.

SAVE THE DATE. WEIRD HAPPENS AGAIN.
MARCH 24-27, 2022   ATLANTA, GA

Limited memberships on sale October 1, 2021

LISTEN ON THIS IS HORROR
TWITTER @THEOUTERDARK
THEOUTERDARK.ORG

Lightning Source UK Ltd.
Milton Keynes UK
UKHW052048101021
391973UK00002B/3